Curiosity killed the

Dorothy, DON'T! she to_____ But it was too late. She had already gone into their room, opened the drawer, and begun to search for whatever it was that had eluded her thoughts that morning.

She stared at her own face in the mirror for a moment. Something is wrong here, in this place, in this house, she told herself. Something is very wrong, I can feel it tingling all around me in the air.

There was a creak on the stairway. . . .

———•———

"I ended the book in goosebumps. Shimmering. Completely entraps the reader."

—*The Washington Post*

SUSPENSE NOVELS BY ROSEMARY WELLS

leave well enough alone

ROSEMARY WELLS

PUFFIN BOOKS

PUFFIN BOOKS

Published by the Penguin Group
Penguin Putnam Books for Young Readers,
345 Hudson Street, New York, New York 10014, U.S.A.
Penguin Books Ltd, 80 Strand, London WC2R ORL, England
Penguin Books Australia Ltd, Ringwood, Victoria, Australia
Penguin Books Canada Ltd, 10 Alcorn Avenue, Toronto, Ontario, Canada M4V 3B2
Penguin Books (N.Z.) Ltd, 182-190 Wairau Road, Auckland 10, New Zealand

Penguin Books Ltd, Registered Offices: Harmondsworth, Middlesex, England

First published in the United States of America by The Dial Press, 1977
Published by Pocket Books, a Simon & Schuster division of Gulf & Western
Corporation, by arrangement with The Dial Press, 1978
Published by Puffin Books,
a division of Penguin Putnam Books for Young Readers, 2002

3 5 7 9 10 8 6 4 2

THE LIBRARY OF CONGRESS HAS CATALOGED THE DIAL EDITION AS FOLLOWS:
Wells, Rosemary.
Leave well enough alone.
Summary: A sheltered fourteen-year-old Catholic girl from a lower middle
class background finds her summer job with a wealthy family a
great strain on her resourcefulness and maturity.
I. Title.
PZ7.W46843Le [Fic] 76-42586
p cm.
ISBN 0-8037-4754-3

Puffin Books ISBN 0-14-230149-3

Printed in the United States of America

For Ginny

One

For fear of appearing terribly stupid, Dorothy had not asked Mrs. Hoade any questions about the directions. She hoped they were right. Mrs. Hoade had written them on the back of a supermarket register tape.

> *Once you get on the spur line in Philadelphia, remember it's the main Philadelphia station, not the Thirtieth Street one, ask the man for the train to Llewellyn. If you get an express, you'll know because it won't stop at Wayne or any of those other places, but it will stop at Llewellyn. If you catch the local, get off at the Monastery stop, which is one station farther down the line*

from Llewellyn but closer for us to pick you up. If you get a local-express, get off at Monastery if it stops there—I can't remember, you'll have to ask the man. And if it doesn't, get off at Llewellyn and call us from the station. I can't tell you which one you're likely to get since they change the schedules every month, it seems, and your train from New York might be late anyway, since they usually are depending on the weather.

If it had been Kate on the phone instead of me, Dorothy told herself, she would have said, "Do you mind going over it once more please, Mrs. Hoade?" As it was, Mrs. Hoade had said, "Were the directions I sent you clear enough, dear?" And Dorothy had answered, "Yes, Mrs. Hoade." And Mrs. Hoade had said, "Well, you have a better head than I do, dear. See you at the Monastery Station."

"Yes, Mrs. Hoade."

"Or the Llewellyn station, as the case may be."

"Yes, Mrs. Hoade."

Dorothy read the instructions again as the Pennsylvania Railroad lumbered unambitiously over the Delaware River bridge. This was her first real summer job. She was to make four hundred dollars for the eight weeks of babysitting. She checked her hair in the window's reflection. The carefully set pageboy she'd combed out that morning had fallen in the heavy July heat. She piled her hair on top of her head for a moment. This emphasized her cheekbones and gave her the look, she liked to think, of Julie Andrews in the new hit musical

My Fair Lady, or perhaps of one of those long-suffering nineteenth-century heroines who threw themselves into the river for love. Making sure no one was observing her, she smiled broadly at her reflection. Then she let down her hair. She was not about to throw herself into the Delaware River. Besides, the fallen pageboy gave her a more dutiful, hardworking look. Her nails were clipped and clean, her penny loafers were, as yet, unscuffed. Her Junior Life Saver badge was sewn to her tank suit, safely placed on top of everything else in her suitcase, so that she could check that it was still there if she wanted.

Mrs. Hoade had shown no familiarity with junior life saving. "Whose life did you save, dear?" she had asked Dorothy with interest, looking at the badge, which was then in Dorothy's wallet.

"Nobody's . . . I mean my best friend Kate's, in practice, but she wasn't really drowning. . . ."

"And they gave you the badge anyway?"

"Well, *if* someone was drowning, I think I could rescue them. I mean I hope I could," said Dorothy hopelessly. "I can manage thirty laps in an Olympic-size . . ."

"I'm sure you would never let Jenny or Lisa drown," said Mrs. Hoade gravely.

Dorothy cast her mind back to that day. The two months that had passed had not quelled her amazement at her good fortune. Sister Margaret McKay had caught her gazing abstractedly at the fig leaf on a statue of Adonis in the foyer of the Frick museum. Sister's glance had been belligerent. Dorothy had dropped her eyes immediately. In dropping them she had noticed something metallic winking at her from behind the pedestal of the statue. She'd waited until Sister busied herself again, purchasing tickets for those students who'd chosen to attend a chamber-music concert instead of sketching one of the paintings. Then she went over and picked the thing up. It was a woman's wallet. It was fat and made of the softest leather she had ever felt. The clasp was large, in the shape of an initial. She wondered if it was solid gold. Inside were five twenty-dollar bills.

"Where'd you get that?" Mary Cudahy, who had been watching Dorothy, asked.

"It was on the floor."

"Better give it to Sister."

"Sister's busy."

"What are you going to do with it?" Mary asked suspiciously, eyeing the money. "Give it to me."

"No. I'm going out to drop it in a mailbox!"

"A mailbox?"

"That's what the law says you're supposed to do with found wallets," Dorothy said. "We had a movie on that. The postman returns it. It's the law."

"It is *not* the law," said Mary, her pale round face reddening righteously under her splotchy freckles. "You're only supposed to drop wallets in mailboxes if you're being pursued by a pickpocket and can't get away." Mary was taller by a head, and surer that she was going to give her life to God than anyone in the class. She looked down her little turned-up nose at everybody. "Give it to me and I'll give it to the guard," she said, reaching for the wallet.

"The guard!" said Dorothy desperately. "You can't give it to the guard. Look at his hands! They're all hairy. I'll bet he has hair all over his body. I wouldn't trust him further than I could throw him! I'm going out and put it in a mailbox."

"Pardon me!" interrupted a very sleek-looking gentleman in a creamy suit "My name is Doctor Zuckerman. I happened to be passing by. Can I do anything to help?"

"We found a wallet," Mary began.

"I found it," said Dorothy.

"This girl found it," amended Mary, her attention on the gentleman. Dorothy took discreet leave of them.

"Dorothy, where are you going?" little Sister Angelica asked, trying to count out quarters from a black silk change purse.

"Out to the mailbox. I won't be a second."

"The concert starts in two and a half minutes!"

"I'm going to sketch instead," said Dorothy.

"Don't get lost!" said Sister Angelica, half hidden by this time in a surging line of students. "Come right back. Don't linger. Remember we're all meeting here at three!" Sister's voice squeaked.

Dorothy found herself out on the street in the early May sunshine. The driver's license and the many charge-account cards listed the wallet's owner, M. Hoade, as living at 143 East Seventy-First Street. Dorothy examined the five crisp twenty-dollar bills. She turned left and walked toward Madison Avenue to find a mailbox. She felt wonderful. The day was as warm and soft as a day could be. Her egg-salad sandwich had withstood the trip from Newburgh, New York, that morning, intact. She had purchased a lovely pin at the United Nations Gift Shop for only three dollars and still had two dollars left. More than anything else, Dorothy felt a surge of pleasure at doing something as plainly honorable as this. On the corner of East Seventy-First and Madison, she found a mailbox. She paused just before she placed the wallet in its iron maw. What if the mailman was not as honest as she? If she walked just a little way farther up the block, she could be sure. M. Hoade would get all the money back. Carefully she fanned out the bills so that the corners just peeked out, in case M. Hoade wanted to give her a spontaneous reward. She bit her lip. That was no way. Doing right was its own reward.

One forty-three was a town house, with a sculpted granite shield over the door. The tiny garden out front was immaculately kept. The brass doorknob and letter slot were polished to such perfection, Dorothy hated to touch the metal. There were two apartments. She rang the bell under the name J. Hoade. The door buzzed and she let herself in.

"Who is it?" called a voice from high up the stairway.

"I found your wallet," Dorothy called back, unable to think of anything else to say.

"Take the elevator," the voice instructed. Then it said, "Oh, dear! I didn't know I'd lost it!"

Dorothy entered the elevator. It was constructed of open brass grillwork and had been made in France in 1910, the little plaque said. She pushed the button and it rose silently, like a birdcage being lifted from a table. What am I doing here? she asked herself suddenly, fearing strangers, remembering her mother's warnings about not talking to anyone in New York City. I don't think you'll be murdered here, Dorothy, she reassured herself as the elevator passed the second floor, which was as richly hung with paintings as the Frick itself. I don't think anyone will steal my two dollars, either. Not in a place like this. Not in broad daylight. Not in 1956.

"How sweet of you!" an apologetic voice said as Dorothy alighted on the third floor. Dorothy found herself face to face with a pleasant-looking woman with widely spaced blue eyes and unkempt brown hair. Her chunky stature was not enhanced by an enormous pregnant stomach.

"I found it in the Frick museum," Dorothy said, handing over the wallet, "behind a statue."

"I must have lost it sitting on a bench this morning," the woman said. "I didn't even notice it was gone. I have so much stuff in my purse, it's always heavy, with or without a wallet." She sighed. "I go to the Frick for rest," she said. "The fountains are so restful. Come in a minute, dear. By the way, I'm Maria Hoade."

Dorothy hesitated. Should I take a chance on something awful happening to me in a stranger's apartment, she asked herself, just because I hope she's going to give me twenty dollars, or even five dollars? She knew dreadful things happened to trusting young girls. Every day of the week innocent young ladies were whisked away and put into the White Slave Market. Dorothy heard an inner voice whisper, Get out, Dorothy, get out while you can.

"Don't worry, please," said Mrs. Hoade, so genuinely that Dorothy paid the inner voice no heed. It would be an insult not to accept just a moment's hospitality. "I'm not going to have the baby now, if you're worried," said Mrs. Hoade with a chuckle.

Once inside, Mrs. Hoade sat down heavily on a seven-foot-long tapestry-covered settee. "I'll get you a Coke," she said, "in a minute. I just want to put my feet up. I thought when you rang the bell you were the maid I'd sent for this morning. I tell you what. The kitchen's over behind there. Help yourself to a Coke by all means. I'm so tired. All I need now is varicose veins."

Dorothy went into the kitchen. "Can I bring you something?" she asked.

"No, dear," said Mrs. Hoade. "Nothing at all. . . . Well, actually you could get me a little glass of sherry. The bottle's in the cabinet over the sink. The glasses are to the right."

Dorothy examined the Coke bottle carefully. Of course it was silly to think someone might have tampered with it, not knowing that she was coming. Still, accepting food or drink from strangers was dangerous. The bottle looked virginal. She came back with the two drinks.

"It's so awful. Thank you, dear," Mrs. Hoade said.

"These people are so undependable. They say they're coming and they never come. I'm just here for the day from Llewellyn. Pennsylvania, that is. I've been down there for most of six months. Before that we've spent nine years in Buenos Aires, can you imagine? John didn't want me to be pregnant in South America. John's my husband, John L. Hoade. So I came back early. We got the girls, Jenny and Lisa, into Miss Parker's School in the city last September. They're boarders and I didn't want to take them out and put them in that awful school in Llewellyn, but I didn't want to be up here all alone pregnant either so I stayed down there. I mean, it would have been the same for them anyway if I'd stayed in Buenos Aires. I've just come up to do the packing. We're going to Llewellyn for the summer and I hired someone to come and help me do the heavy stuff and now they're three hours late and I know they're not coming at all."

Dorothy nodded, wide-eyed, at Mrs. Hoade's rambling account and stared at the splendid furniture, paintings, and rugs in the apartment. She tried to drink her Coke as noiselessly as she could. She sat with her back erect and kept her feet together. Unfortunately, Mrs. Hoade seemed to have forgotten about the wallet. She hadn't even counted the money.

"Dear," said Mrs. Hoade, her eyes fastened on the gold cross that hung against the front of Dorothy's navy-blue uniform jumper. "You would be an absolute saint if you'd get up on a chair and take down the two valises in the bedroom closet. I'm afraid to do it. I'm eight and a half months."

At two o'clock, after an hour and a half had passed, Dorothy was exhausted. She'd helped herself to another Coke. She had retrieved the suitcases, plus three other large ones from under the bed. She'd sorted two huge piles of clothes and hung twenty-two little-girls' dresses in the cedar closet. She'd made two beds and packed three huge cartons full of toys and books. Mrs. Hoade, to her dismay, had not once mentioned the wallet or gone over to where it lay on the coffee table. Instead she'd twittered on about taking care of the girls' sick great-grandmother in Llewellyn, the difficulties in getting reliable household help, and the awfulness of pregnancy. Dorothy had the distinct impression that Mr. Hoade was going to leave Mrs. Hoade if the baby was not a boy.

"Look at that!" Mrs. Hoade said, coming to a dead stop in the midst of sorting great numbers of mismatched socks into senselessly arranged groupings and then dropping them all in a forlorn heap in the middle of the bed.

"What?" asked Dorothy.

"It kicked. It doesn't kick very much, I'm afraid. Put your hand right there!" With excruciating loathing, Dorothy touched Mrs. Hoade's stomach lightly. She felt a small movement under the maternity smock and withdrew her hand instantly. "See!" said Mrs. Hoade. "I think that was an elbow. It only kicks once in a great while. I'm worried. Both girls kicked horribly. I'm sure something's wrong but the doctors never tell you anything. I go to Mamie Eisenhower's gynecologist, but I'm sure he looks after Mamie better than he does me."

"Have you ever seen her in the waiting room?" Dorothy asked, hoping to steer Mrs. Hoade away from the topic of babies.

"Mrs. Eisenhower doesn't wait in waiting rooms," Mrs. Hoade said sadly. "I'm sure they fly the doctor right down to the White House and do the whole thing in the Lincoln Bedroom."

Dorothy cleared her throat. "I'll have to be going," she said. "I have to get back to my class trip before they find out I'm gone." She thought regretfully about the wallet. Try as she might, she had not been able to introduce that topic back into conversation. I know it's retribution, she thought, for being greedy and wanting a reward instead of letting God reward me with His love and approval.

"Dear," said Mrs. Hoade suddenly, "how would you like a job?"

"A job! But I live in Newburgh, New York."

"I mean for the summer."

"The summer?"

"I had a girl lined up months ago. A mother's helper. You know, from the Anne Carpenter people? A college girl. She was lovely. A week ago I got a letter from her saying she was going to Europe instead. The little . . . In any case, I'm stuck, as you can see. The agency can't promise me anyone at this late date and I hate to take a chance on another debutante anyway. Can you swim?"

The figure of four hundred dollars now flickered briefly in Dorothy's imagination. She thought, perhaps, come next Labor Day she would stand in the middle of her room and throw all four hundred dollar bills into the air and shout Wahoo! Of course it all had to go into the bank. She might have been able to keep a hundred of it if it hadn't been for Stanley Inglewasser and her sister, Maureen.

"May you burn in hell, Stanley!" Dorothy allowed herself this wish for the fiftieth time since "it" had happened. "It" had happened smack in the middle of Reverend Mother's opening prayer at the Senior Awards Assembly. Dorothy's older brother, Terrance, had been about to receive the Boys' Good Citizenship Medal. It would be announced, also, that he had won an athletic scholarship to Holy Cross. A beaming, fidgeting Terrance sat upon the stage with the other award winners, flanked by the Boys' Glee Club and the Girls' Choir, behind formidable, six-foot-three Mother Superior, whose vast white flowing habit and hawklike eyes gave the impression of a terrifying, magic bird.

Stanley had passed her the note at the beginning of the assembly. Dorothy hadn't looked at it until she was sure Reverend Mother's eyes were tightly closed in prayer, but when the opening prayer was over, Reverend Mother had inclined her head slightly, and like a bullfrog snapping up a fly on a remote leaf, she'd said, *Dorothy Coughlin!* in a tone that could have shattered marble. "You will read to the assembly whatever that note contains since it takes such precedence over our prayers."

Dorothy could remember her Latin book sliding off her lap, hitting the floor with a slap that made several

people giggle in nervous appreciation. She could remember wishing she could go into a six-hour faint so
that everyone would think she was near death, but she
only managed to shake. Her hands, particularly. Looking at the quivering paper, she'd nearly whispered, "Meet
. . . meet me after school at the bus stop." There were
snickers.

"No one can hear you," Reverend Mother responded.
"Please come up and read it from the podium, Dorothy."

Hundreds of faces watched Dorothy. Open-mouthed
and unsmiling they rose before her and then receded
like an ocean wave. She wondered if they'd all heard
her say "Excuse me, excuse me," at least a dozen times
as she'd made her way from her seat to the stage. She
wondered how many heard her say "I'll meet you after
school at the bus stop," in almost as soft a voice as she'd
used before. The titters were general.

"You read it differently this time, Dorothy," Reverend
Mother commented evenly. "The first time you said,
'Meet me.' The second time you said, 'I'll meet you.'
Perhaps you'd better let me see the note."

Reverend Mother plucked the miserable, damp piece
of notebook paper from Dorothy's hands. She indicated
Dorothy should stand down, and adjusting her steel-
rimmed bifocals, she glanced at the door at the end of the
auditorium, as if she were about to announce a pep rally,
and read out, "Cicero or Caesar, question mark." Then
she looked over at Dorothy. "To what does this refer,
Dorothy?" she asked.

"I'm not sure, Reverend Mother." Reverend Mother's

tongue slipped out between her perfect, dull white teeth. Teeth Dorothy'd never had the stomach to look at because they were false and occasionally lost their position in Reverend Mother's mouth. Reverend Mother waited for Dorothy's reply.

"It refers to the Latin final, I guess," said Dorothy at last, her eyes avoiding everything in the room.

"The examination you just took?"

"Yes, Reverend Mother."

"The same examination Freshman Latin section two is to take sixth period this afternoon?"

"Yes, Reverend Mother."

"I see." More silence. No one giggled now. Dorothy had once turned to look at the audience behind her in the middle of the scariest part of *The Creature from the Black Lagoon*. The expressions in front of her were similar to those. "And who do you think sent you this note, Dorothy?"

"I'm not sure, Reverend Mother."

"It looks like Stanley Inglewasser's handwriting to me."

"Yes. Yes, well it probably was . . . him."

"He."

"He."

"Stanley is to take that examination sixth period, I believe. Had you intended to reply to his question?"

"No, Reverend Mother."

"I see."

"Reverend Mother, it wasn't *my* fault. I never . . ."

"You and Stanley will see me after Assembly. You

may take your seat. We shall continue the program. I believe your brother Terrance is the first to be honored."

Reverend Mother's interview was painful enough. She announced at the conclusion that Dorothy's and Stanley's mothers had been asked to come in at three o'clock.

Reverend Mother kept Dorothy and Stanley waiting in the foyer of her office for exactly fifteen minutes while she spoke first with Mrs. Inglewasser and then with Dorothy's mother. Dorothy did not once look at Stanley. She tried to hear what Reverend Mother was saying, but Reverend Mother's door was too thick. Dorothy sat in as stiff and prim a posture as she could manage, as if to ward off the rays of terrible power that seemed to emanate from Reverend Mother's office. Stanley, on the other hand, kept one ankle cocked over his knee, showing a dirty white cotton sock. He slouched, and needed only a cigarette between his fingers to appear as if he were simply waiting for a bus.

Dorothy's mother said nothing when she emerged from the office. She nodded to Mrs. Inglewasser, who for some reason was still in the foyer, standing between Dorothy and Stanley as if she didn't quite know what to do. Since Reverend Mother had closed the door without coming out again, Mrs. Inglewasser did sigh as if something had been completed, and the four of them walked down the darkened corridor to the big double doors that led to daylight at the end. No one said a word. Four pairs of shoes echoed hideously on the shiny waxed floor.

Her own mother's humiliation and disappointment

were unbearable to Dorothy, but it had been Maureen who'd made her feel like a criminal.

Plain Maureen with her baby, her migraines, her dandruff shampoo, her Jergens Lotion and her Nair for the upper lip. Maureen was twenty and she was already married and had corns. Corns! And special shoes! That evening, when Dorothy's family gathered for what turned out to be a rather glum celebration of Terrance's success, Maureen had observed airily that she supposed Dorothy would no longer be taking her fancy-pants job in Pennsylvania. Maureen thought that would be an excellent penance.

Dorothy's eyes had filled with tears. She watched her father's and mother's faces across the table, under the dim kitchen ceiling light. Maureen thought Dorothy ought to take a job as a volunteer candy striper in the Veteran's Hospital. After all, hadn't Reverend Mother suggested some sort of penance? It was the four hundred dollars that had saved Dorothy in the end. Maureen couldn't argue with money. "You've disgraced your family," she insisted. "With Daddy on the force and Arthur on the force and Terrance winning the medal! It's a disgrace. Worse, it's a mortal sin."

Dorothy's father was a sergeant on the Newburgh police force. Maureen's husband, Arthur, was a patrolman. Arthur didn't look terribly disgraced to Dorothy. His mouth was too full of meatloaf. Her father just appeared puzzled.

"That doesn't mean I have to give up four hundred dollars which I intend to use for my college education,"

Dorothy had shot back. Her father's wiry gray eyebrows had lifted at this and he'd exchanged glances with Dorothy's mother.

"Then how do you intend to atone for what you've done? Reverend Mother told Mom that she'd told you that you have to atone for what you've done," said Maureen.

"I have to take the Latin exam over again in September."

"That's not enough. Stanley was failed and has to take the whole year of Latin again. Besides, Latin's always been a cinch for you."

"*Stanley* sent the note, Maureen. I didn't even answer it."

"You were going to, though. Weren't you? If you hadn't been caught red-handed. I know you have a picture of him in your wallet that Judy Dugan gave you. I know you go four blocks out of your way every afternoon after school on your bicycle just to see Stanley's chest when he takes his shirt off when he mows his neighbors' lawns. It's indecent!"

"That's enough, Maureen," Dorothy's father had interrupted at that moment and Dorothy knew she'd won.

"It isn't fair!" Maureen had cried.

"What isn't fair?" Dorothy asked in a newly confident voice.

This time Maureen's eyes had filled. "It isn't fair because she gets everything. She always has. She's a spoiled brat. She gets away with murder." Maureen threw down her napkin. "She's going to wind up in jail someday.

You wait!" Maureen left the room to tend Bridget, the baby, who was by this time howling.

"Come visit me if I do!" Dorothy had trilled merrily after her sister. "And bring me a cake with a knife in it so I can escape and come home and baby-sit for you which is all you want."

"Shut up," said Arthur. "You know she's pregnant." That was the first and only thing Arthur said all evening.

"You shut up," said Terrance. "Dorothy's right." Dorothy's father observed that he didn't like the word shut up.

Thank heaven Stanley had had the brains to wash off Dorothy's initials before they'd gone in to see Reverend Mother. When she'd seen them, tattooed to his hand in ballpoint pen, before the assembly, her heart or her stomach or whatever it was in her middle had turned over in ecstasy. Now, as her train pulled in to the Thirtieth Street Station, the one she was not supposed to disembark at, that same organ turned over again, but in a sad, stinging way. Dorothy had explained to Reverend Mother that she'd felt guilty about getting someone else into trouble and was therefore, by the dictates of her conscience, obliged to lie about the contents of the note for moral reasons. Reverend Mother could not recall a lie having been told for moral reasons under any conditions save those in wartime, but perhaps she had detected some ember of innocence behind Dorothy's tearful words and so she was easier on her than she might have been. With Stanley, Reverend Mother had shown no mercy. Not only did he have to repeat a year's work but she obliged him to clean and polish every inch of statuary in the church.

Dorothy squeezed her eyes shut to make the evil feeling vanish. It was clear why Stanley, who'd never before given her the time of day, had written her initials on his hand. He just wanted the answers to the exam. She'd lied to protect him because of it. She would try to atone. But she'd never tell anyone even if she did find a way. She opened her eyes again and fastened them on the sign that said "Thirtieth Street." That's where I don't get off, she told herself as the sign began to pull behind the slowly moving train. Another sign beyond said Thirtieth Street again. A mistake *not* made, said Dorothy, trying to cheer herself up.

Premeditated lying was, of course, a mortal sin, but supposing one lied in simple reaction without thinking? When Mrs. Hoade had asked her how old she was she'd answered right away, "Fifteen," which was what she'd be in October, after all. She guessed the sin would not be wiped out in October. When Mrs. Hoade had asked her if she had brothers and sisters, Dorothy had said, "Oh, yes, two brothers and a sister," which was quite true. However, she hadn't mentioned that she was the youngest and had no experience whatever in taking care of children. Mrs. Hoade had simply replied that large families were nice, and that Dorothy looked older than fifteen. Dorothy had thanked Mrs. Hoade. Her own mother had been very dubious about an inexperienced fourteen-year-old taking a job in Pennsylvania, six hours from home, but Dorothy had worked on her father, who knew how much she dreaded a summer alone with Maureen. Her parents, Dorothy reasoned, probably felt a little guilty about going off to Ireland for the whole summer by themselves, the first time they'd been on vacation alone since their honeymoon in Atlantic City, twenty-five years before. They were going to visit Dorothy's other brother, Kevin, who was studying for the priesthood somewhere in the west of Ireland. Mercifully, Dorothy's mother had seemed to like Mrs. Hoade's voice when Mrs. Hoade had called up to reaffirm her offer of a job, and to assure Mrs. Coughlin that Dorothy would be safe. Her mother had not volunteered the information that Dorothy was inexperienced with children—which was unusual, because Dorothy's mother was so scrupulously honest that she put dimes back in vending machines and telephones that gave more change than they ought. "A telephone is not a slot machine," she'd told a dismayed Dorothy on more than one occasion.

Dorothy felt a little queasy about the whole subject of children. She had smiled with relief when Mrs. Hoade informed her that she herself would take care of the new baby.

"I can see you're sorry not to have charge of the little one, too," she'd said with such stunning inaccuracy that Dorothy immediately stopped smiling, "but you'll be able to hold her, or him, from time to time, if you like. I do hope it's a boy. John so much wants a boy after two girls."

The last time Dorothy had held an infant, she'd lifted Bridget gingerly from her bassinette, only to have

Bridget throw up all over her shoulder. Dorothy had nearly tossed the baby back to Maureen and had made a beeline for the bathroom, where she'd gotten sick herself. She'd left her blouse, a new one, in Maureen's wastebasket. It was too bad, but she knew she'd never be able to look at that blouse again without thinking of Bridget and that ghastly smell.

After checking the signs, Dorothy alighted at the main station. She lugged her suitcase onto the platform and set it down with a thud, sending a large run down the length of her left stocking. Oh, no, she thought, I don't dare take the time to find a ladies' room in case I miss my train. I wonder if they have ladies' rooms on little local trains? Maybe I'll just buy a newspaper and spread it over my knees. That way I can take the stockings off underneath it and no one will see.

A porter stepped solemnly up to her suitcase, lifted it onto his dolly, and broke the handle. "What have you got in that thing? Rocks?" he asked.

Dorothy had not expected a porter. "I think I can manage it, thank you," she said.

"Not with no handle, you can't," said the porter defiantly. He turned around and trundled off down the platform with it.

Dorothy ran after him. "Can I ask you how much you charge?" she said miserably to the shiny twill back. "Because I have only ten dollars left and . . ."

"That should do it," said the porter, not looking back at her. "Where to? Cab? Hotel?"

"Llewellyn. I'm to make a connection for Llewellyn." Dorothy stopped at a newsstand. She was determined not to ask the porter for change of a five-dollar bill in case he didn't have any change and became angry and either kept the five dollars or hurled her suitcase onto the tracks.

"A pack of cigarettes, please, and this paper," she asked the mustachioed proprietress. The woman turned a pair of sightless blue eyes on Dorothy.

"What kind?" she asked.

Was it against the law in Pennsylvania for a minor to buy cigarettes? Dorothy asked herself. Thank heaven the woman was blind. "Camels, please," she said, lowering her voice an octave. "Here's a five-dollar bill. I'm sorry I have nothing smaller."

The woman fingered the money. How can she tell the difference? Dorothy wondered, as the silver and four ones appeared before her in a little wooden tray. Camels were what Kathleen's father smoked and what she and Kate had sneaked, two at a time, out of his pack to puff on down in the cellar. Kate was also well supplied with Sen-Sen.

"And a package of Sen-Sen, please," said Dorothy, handing over another dollar.

"I jes' give you two quarters," said the woman.

"I'm sorry, but I need that for the porter," said Dorothy, with panicky certainty that she'd never see the porter or her suitcase again. The woman spat on the floor but gave Dorothy change all the same.

"Thank you," Dorothy shouted as if the woman had been deaf as well and she clattered down the platform as fast as she could, as much to escape the woman's unseeing eyes as to catch up with her belongings.

"Dorothy is *very* bright," Sister Elizabeth MacIntosh's last term report rang in her ears, as she flew down a dirty set of stairs after the porter's disappearing back. "But she lacks *discipline, organization,* and *concentration.* Let's hope for an improvement next year!" Usually, Sister quoted Shakespeare or Sir Walter Scott, underscoring words freely so that the point would not escape a student, and giving, if possible, the source of the quote down to the year it was written. "I wish, Dorothy," Sister had remarked in one of her many marginal notes on a composition paper, "that you had the *stoicism* of your sister Maureen, the *application* of your brother Terrance, and the *humility* of your brother Kevin, because your brain is better and your *potential superior* to any of them. *Please stop dropping participles!* 'He will guide the mild in judgment: He will teach the *meek* His ways!' Psalm 24, v.9."

The porter set the suitcase down and held out his hand. Dorothy placed two quarters in it. The fingers curled over the money, but the hand did not drop. Dorothy gave him two more quarters. "Is this the local, the local-express, or the express?" she asked as mildly as she could.

"Express," said the porter and vanished down the platform at an astonishing clip.

Dorothy struggled to lift her now handleless suitcase into the train. She did not attempt to get it into the overhead rack, and hoped the conductor wouldn't object to its being in the aisle. Underneath her clothes, the suitcase was filled with books she was supposed to have finished by the end of the summer. Sister Elizabeth taught all four years of Section 1 English at Sacred Heart Academy. She admonished her students to "turn lazy hours in the sun into golden ones" by filling the minutes with Dickens or Twain or her favorite—and Dorothy's least favorite—Sir Walter Scott. Dorothy spread the paper over her knees. No one had yet entered the train. She removed both stockings quickly but didn't dare try and take off her garter belt in case someone did come in and had her arrested for indecent exposure. She tapped a Camel out of the pack and slipped a copy of *The Case of the Complacent Corpse* out of her pocketbook. She knew she wouldn't read *Nicholas Nickelby* by Labor Day.

Just you wait! She told invisible Sister Elizabeth. Someday you'll see. Dorothy pictured that on just such an occasion as this, when she was alone in a train and no one could overhear, a man in a trench coat or a woman in a blue serge suit would come up and whisper that Scotland Yard or the CIA or perhaps even the French Sureté had been scouting her for years and wanted to recruit her. Whatever agency it was, her talents would be recognized and she would be sent on dangerous missions in East Germany. Perhaps she would come back to Newburgh one day and meet Sister Elizabeth on the street. "Dorothy!" Sister would exclaim. "It's been so many years! I expect you're married now with a family, just like Maureen!" "No," Dorothy would say, taking a Players Oval from a steel cigarette case. "As a matter of fact, I've just gotten back from Berlin. Can't talk about it, of course. It's all hush-hush. If I meet with an accident, give my best to Reverend Mother." And Dorothy would slip off into the fog leaving Sister with her mouth open, her eyes agog, and her Walter Scott waiting to be said.

"Little lady, where are you going?" a kindly white-haired conductor asked, peering in the door of the train.

"Llewellyn, I think," said Dorothy stamping out the cigarette hastily.

"Well, you'd better get in the train opposite then," he instructed, looking sadly at the dangling handle on her suitcase. "This one's going to Atlanta in a few hours." He lifted the suitcase with both arms and grunted, "We don't want you winding up in Atlanta, do we?"

"Oh, please," Dorothy protested, "I can carry it, I really can."

"What have you got in here, rocks?" he asked, setting it down again with a thud.

"Books," said Dorothy miserably.

"Books!" said the conductor gasping. "Well, I guess you're not a juvenile delinquent then, eh? I hope you read them after all this. Those yours?" he added, pointing to the stockings, which Dorothy had dropped on the floor like hated things.

"No," said Dorothy.

Twenty pairs of eyes followed Dorothy and the conductor down the aisle of the new train. He put the suitcase in an overhead rack and Dorothy handed him a crumpled dollar bill. "Wouldn't dream of it," he said, rather too loudly for her comfort. "Hope it's all clean books," he added, with a leer at the lurid cover of *The Case of the Complacent Corpse*.

"It's really Dickens and Twain and Scott," said Dorothy, but the conductor was no longer listening. "All aboard!" he shouted in the middle of her word Twain.

Dorothy took a seat. To her dismay, one of her discarded stockings had somehow attached itself to the hinge of her suitcase. The conductor had set the suitcase down for a second after his first attempt to lift it. No doubt he'd set it down on one of the stockings. Now it had freed itself and hung down from the overhead rack like some dreadful nylon boa. She would have to do something. She stood up and yanked it off and jammed it angrily into her pocket. Everyone in the train watched. Get organized now! she scolded herself under her breath. She looked again at the instructions Mrs. Hoade had given her.

"Llewellyn, I guess," she said when the conductor came back to take her ticket.

"Now make up your mind, honey. Is someone going to meet you at the station?"

"No, I'm to phone them," said Dorothy. "Llewellyn, then."

The train made stops at Wayne and Bryn Mawr. This can't be the express, she told herself, but I'd better get off at Llewellyn anyway since I've paid for it and he'll think I'm hopeless if I change my mind.

To Dorothy's surprise, she saw Mrs. Hoade waiting for her at the Llewellyn station as the train pulled in. The conductor followed Dorothy to the door of the train and helped her once again with her suitcase. He gave her a smile and pat on the arm. "Dropped something," he said as she descended to the platform. It was the stocking.

"So lovely to see you, dear," Mrs. Hoade said, grappling with Dorothy's suitcase. "What happened to the handle?"

"It . . . came off," said Dorothy.

"Dear, where are the girls?" Mrs. Hoade added immediately as the train pulled out. "Where are the girls?"

"The girls?"

"Didn't I tell you to look for them on the train? They were on the same train with you. Didn't I tell you to look for them? Let me see my instructions."

Dorothy handed over the register tape, praying the instructions to look for Mrs. Hoade's daughters had not magically appeared since she had looked at it last. Mrs. Hoade's lips moved as she read her own handwriting. "You're right," she said. "No matter . . . the school promised to put large tags on them with hard-to-open diaper pins. Besides, Jenny knows to get off at Monastery if she by any chance missed you. I talked to the headmistress last night. We'll have to rush to catch up with the train. No dear, don't use that door. It hasn't opened for months. Get in my side."

Dorothy crawled across the seat of the very dirty old black Ford. Mrs. Hoade jumped in after managing to get

Dorothy's suitcase into the trunk. She pumped the accelerator vigorously. "This hasn't worked properly in months, either," she said. "There's something about getting a car fixed that I can't stand." She ground the gears horribly and lurched through a ditch onto the road. Mrs. Hoade ran her fingers through her hair nervously, like a man, Dorothy thought. Her old linen skirt was creased, and despite the heat she wore a sleeveless woolen pullover. It had been put on inside out. Without her pregnant stomach, Mrs. Hoade was still squarish in shape; Dorothy decided Mrs. Hoade might have been pretty enough if she could lose fifty pounds and do something about her hair and clothes.

"I'm sure you're wondering why I'm wearing this sweater inside out," said Mrs. Hoade, taking note of Dorothy's eyes, which had fastened on the stray threads along her shoulder. "It's a long story." The speedometer hit forty and then fifty. Her face broke into a grin as she steered the car over the wildly rutted road. There were no houses here, Dorothy noticed, at least none she could see behind the hedges and stone entrance gates that occasionally appeared by the roadside. All that was visible to her were woods and meadows full of daisies and black-eyed Susans. The parched sandy gulleys on either side of the road were overgrown with intimidating-looking thistles.

"Excuse me," said Dorothy. "But shouldn't we follow that other road along the tracks if we want to catch the train?"

"This is a shortcut," said Mrs. Hoade.

"You were saying about . . . inside out?"

"Oh, yes. I knitted this thing from a complicated pattern in the *Vogue* book, you know," Mrs. Hoade went on, "and I didn't see until I was almost finished that I'd knitted the initials in the book instead of my own. Can you imagine? But it was too late. I can't very well go around in a sweater that says *PEN* instead of *MCH*, so I wear it inside out." The Ford hit a particularly deep pothole. "Are you uncomfortable, dear?" asked Mrs. Hoade speeding up again as soon as the rear axle had dislodged itself from the macadam.

"No, I'm fine," said Dorothy. The catch on her loose garter belt was biting into her leg.

"I'll teach you to drive this summer, dear, if you like," said Mrs. Hoade kindly.

"But I'm only . . . fifteen. I won't be able to have even a learner's permit until I'm . . ."

"Never mind. The police never pick up anybody on these roads. I learned when I was eleven. Went right through the hedge the first time. The car stuck in the middle of the hedge and I couldn't go backward or forward!" Dorothy gave what she hoped was an appropriate gasp of horror. "Never laughed so much in my life," said Mrs. Hoade. "But I'm a good driver. Fast but good. I'll teach you how to shift gears. Then you'll find one of those automatics a breeze."

"I couldn't," said Dorothy. "If my father found out he'd absolutely die."

"Why, dear?"

"Well, he's a policeman."

"A policeman!" said Mrs. Hoade in a particularly explosive voice. The left wheels spun hideously around a right curve. Then she added, "Well, of course. You are Irish."

"I know. And I have the map of Ireland on my face," said Dorothy more resentfully than she'd intended.

"Oh, dear. I didn't mean it that way. I think it's wonderful that he's a policeman. It's just that you hadn't mentioned it and it took me by surprise and I have a habit of blurting out whatever's on my mind at the moment. I'm terribly sorry!"

"Well, I *am* proud of my Dad," said Dorothy after a pause. "He's Chief of Police of Newburgh, New York. My brother-in-law, Arthur, is on the force too. He's the head of the crime lab. He used to be a detective before they promoted him."

"What an accomplished family!"

"My brother's going to law school. He'll probably go into criminal law one day."

"Is he at Harvard or Yale?"

"Holy Cross."

"That's even better!" said Mrs. Hoade in such a desperate voice that Dorothy felt sorry for her. She was trying to say something nice. Dorothy decided not to be angry.

"Haven't you ever done something like that?" Mrs. Hoade asked miserably. "Say with an Italian? Said something like 'How thin you look! How do you manage with all that spaghetti?' "

"Yes," said Dorothy. She had, after all, almost called

Stanley Inglewasser a dirty kraut after the interview with Reverend Mother. "I guess everybody does."

"Good then. Am I forgiven?"

"Of *course!*" said Dorothy. She really wanted to give poor anxious Mrs. Hoade a hug.

"Thank you," said Mrs. Hoade humbly. "Whenever I think of the Irish, I think of Yeats."

Dorothy thought she'd change the subject before Mrs. Hoade went on to list Saint Patrick and Hopalong Cassidy. "How's the baby?" she asked with as much enthusiasm as she could muster. "I bet it's just as cute as . . . anything!"

"I was just going to say something about that," said Mrs. Hoade. The speedometer hit sixty-five. Why does she drive so fast if it makes her sweat so much? Dorothy wondered, as the Ford careened around another blind curve. "She was born a mongoloid. Have you ever heard of . . ."

"You mean one of those—"

"That's exactly what I mean," said Mrs. Hoade. "Now, Dorothy. I want this understood. Lisa, our nine-year-old, is very impressionable. She has nightmares and suffers from enuresis—"

"What's *that*?" interrupted Dorothy.

"Well, she wets her bed occasionally." Dorothy stopped herself just in time from saying *Oh no!* She tried to look interested, instead, in the ailments of the new baby. Mrs. Hoade was going on about not bothering the nurse, who was taking care of it. And not going down to the cottage where it was living.

"Oh, you don't have to worry about that," said Dorothy, wondering whether "occasionally" meant every night or every other night. The prospect of changing wet sheets determined her, at that moment, never to let Lisa within a mile of whatever cottage Mrs. Hoade was talking about. Poor Mrs. Hoade. The whole subject of her baby evidently distressed her very much. There was unmistakable shame and guilt in Mrs. Hoade's voice. Dorothy tried to think of something cheerful to say. "Please don't think I think anything bad about it," she began, noticing a vein throbbing in Mrs. Hoade's left temple. "I mean, I was almost a mongoloid too."

"What on earth do you mean, dear? Almost a mongoloid?"

"Well, my mother was forty when she had me. She told me I could easily have been one."

"Forty! My goodness. What about your brothers and sisters? She must have been worried about them."

Dorothy breathed deeply. "Well, I guess I didn't mention it, but they're all . . . older."

"No young ones in the family?"

"I'm afraid not, Mrs. Hoade. I didn't mean to lie. I guess I just didn't say anything because you didn't ask. I wanted the job so much. I suppose I'd better tell you I'm not terribly experienced with children."

"Well, my goodness," said Mrs. Hoade.

"Are you angry?" asked Dorothy immediately.

"Do you think you can manage?"

"Of course, Mrs. Hoade."

"Say no more then," said Mrs. Hoade.

Dorothy stared out the window. She heard the diesel whistle somewhere behind the next hill. For the first time she noticed how lovely the softly rolling hills were, how peaceful and reassuring the old farms looked. She wished to jump out of the car and run right through the nearest meadow. She wished her family lived in a place like this.

Two small figures sat on the only bench at the Monastery station. They swung their legs and slouched, evidently unperturbed by what to Dorothy was a very menacing-looking building, even in the daylight. The station had been long closed, it appeared. Its windows and door were boarded over and weeds straggled through the cracked platform. The wood-shingled roof did not incline on an even plane but undulated slightly, like a woman's hat. The eaves, at least two feet deep, overshadowed the blinded windows. How she would have identified the station, had she stayed on the train to this stop, Dorothy didn't know, for the single sign had long faded into illegibility. Mrs. Hoade screeched to a halt. At least the brakes worked on this car, Dorothy thought.

Four hundred dollars, she reminded herself again, after riding in the car with Jenny and Lisa for several minutes. Jenny, a doleful, pear-shaped child with dull blond hair and a sallow complexion, had not said hello. She'd only stared at Dorothy's extended hand and announced that she was eleven years old and that her sister was nine. Lisa, a much livelier specimen, had corrected this to nine and a half, and the two of them argued the exactitudes of their respective ages until Mrs. Hoade interrupted with questions about school. Dorothy did not listen. She felt like an intruder. She wished they would just disappear. She found herself thinking she'd discovered her penance.

When the subject of Miss Parker's third grade and Miss Parker's fifth grade had been exhausted, Jenny asked, "How's the kid? Still sick?"

"It has a very bad cold," said Mrs. Hoade.

"That's a pretty long cold," Lisa commented. Dorothy bit her lip. She was not the only person inclined to palatable half-truths in this world.

"Now I don't want you going down to bother the nurse or the baby," said Mrs. Hoade. "All we need is to have you catch—"

"Don't worry," said Lisa. "How's Great-grandma?"

"She's off on a visit," said Mrs. Hoade cheerfully. Somehow Dorothy could tell instantly that this was another lie.

"How could she be off on a visit if she was so sick?"

"She's much better now," said Mrs. Hoade. Mrs. Hoade drove as if she had to catch another train. Dorothy watched the speedometer.

"Who's she visiting?" Lisa asked.

"She's visiting friends at a lovely place called Crest-view."

"Sounds like a nuthouse," Jenny said.

"It happens to be a first-class, top-drawer . . . well, resort, almost, for elderly people who want to have a little vacation."

"Oh, *Mom*," Jenny drawled.

"I don't want to be late. We're having a party tonight," Mrs. Hoade explained to Dorothy, noticing Dorothy's position, which was not unlike that of a rider in a roller coaster. "You're perfectly safe with me. I know these roads. I used to be a dangerous driver, I guess," she went on. "But John, my husband, made me slow down the minute I married him. I haven't gotten a speeding ticket in twelve years."

"That's nice," said Dorothy, not releasing her viselike grip on the armrest beside her.

"He's a wonderful man. You'll like him very very much, I'm sure."

Dorothy noticed the tension that had crept into Mrs. Hoade's voice at the mention of her husband. What a curious woman, Dorothy thought. Mrs. Hoade bore not the slightest resemblance to anyone else's mother, to any of the Sisters at school, even to lay teachers. There was an irreverence about her laughter that Dorothy found shocking in an adult. She was reminded of something her mother had said late one night when they were finishing up a pile of dishes. "All I ever did at your age, Dotty, was laugh, just like you and Kate. Enjoy these years. They come to an end soon enough."

"But you laugh too, Mom," Dorothy had said, frightened suddenly.

"I laugh. But it isn't the same."

The Hoades were rich. That much Dorothy could tell from their New York apartment. Did that mean that Mrs. Hoade could go right on laughing all her life? Did she never have to worry about discipline and organization and humility? The car slowed down at last and turned into a long driveway filled with fallen yellow willow leaves. At the end of the driveway was the biggest house Dorothy had ever seen. Homesickness overcame her for a moment. She missed the small kitchen at home with the church calendar that still showed January because no one ever bothered to turn the pages. She missed her mother and her mother's smooth, white, manicured hands that looked as if they never touched dishwater. "Always take care of your hands. People will judge you by them," her mother advised. Dorothy noticed Mrs. Hoade's hands were red, the nails bitten and uncared for. Surely Mrs. Hoade didn't do laundry and floors. And why did she dress so poorly? She was as disheveled as Mrs. Kroll, down at the end of Dorothy's street. She's married a rich man, Dorothy concluded. But she's kept a lot of bad old habits like not dressing well, not taking pride in her appearance. Just like Polly Kroll, who never wore a clean uniform to school and whose brothers and sisters were always running around looking disgusting and saying dirty words. Dorothy decided that if she were ever to marry a rich man, she would have no trouble at all adjusting to an expensive wardrobe and would immediately start acting as if she'd been rich all her life.

Chapter

Two

"Mind the bees," said a voice. Dorothy looked up. A tall man in a blue blazer was grinning at her. He held a drink in each hand. His silk shirt was opened down three buttons to allow a curly tangle of hair to be seen on his chest. He was deeply suntanned and except for his bent-in teeth, he looked like a movie star. Dorothy thought he was a movie star.

"No, thank you," she said to the drink.

The man gestured to the phlox and roses that grew at the base of the nearest stucco arch. A few sleepy bees hovered unthreateningly. "I'm John Hoade. You must be the new girl."

"Well, thank you," she said, feeling she ought to accept the drink. She could at least hold it and look polite. "I'm Dorothy Coughlin," she added. "Pleased to meet you, sir." Dorothy was very grateful that Mr. Hoade took the conversation from there, as she couldn't think of a single other thing to say.

He was so strange. Everything was so strange. Strange and wonderful. The pool, for example. Instead of a concrete rectangle painted aquamarine blue, the Hoades' swimming pool was oval and made entirely of white tile with a colored mosaic of zodiac signs around the inside. The water was limpid, inviting. It was clear, of course, and looked like . . . Dorothy paused in the middle of this train of thought . . . like real water instead of the unnatural vibrant-blue fluid in the pool at the YMCA. "Thank you for the drink, sir," said Dorothy as Mr. Hoade moved off, smiling. Evidently he too had run out of things to say.

Dorothy sat down on the nearest chair, careful to gather her best cotton dress up beneath as she did, careful to keep her legs together. Careful to smile as if she didn't notice not talking to anyone. She didn't mind, really. She wanted to consider these surroundings for the moment. She sniffed at the nearly colorless liquid that swirled around the olive in the small conical glass Mr. Hoade had given her. She didn't think she'd sip it. The odor was too powerful. She guessed it was gin. Dorothy knew the difference between the smells and colors of gin and whiskey. She and Kate had inhaled from Mrs. Codd's empty liquor bottles on the stoop next to Kate's house. To their disappointment neither she nor Kate had ever gotten drunk in this fashion although Kate's younger brother said you could.

The people around her, laughing and chattering away with each other, were not costumed in togas or gold lamé bodices. They were not lying on their backs consuming great quantities of grapes and wine. No one was holding a lance or a torch or a spear, but they might as well have been for the impression they made upon Dorothy.

The pool itself was surrounded by stucco arches, each of these covered with Virginia creeper in tender scarlet-and-green leaf. The pool house and the four cabanas that stood beside it were fronted with miniature Doric columns, that was why she thought of Ancient Rome. There were no tacky folding awning-cloth chairs here. All the furniture was heavy wicker, and had been painted with shiny white enamel. A bartender in a brilliant red jacket stood a little way off, polishing crystal glasses. Dorothy watched him. Someone backed into the bar, knocking a glass to the floor, shattering it on the frosty-white tiles. The person looked down for a moment and then resumed talking. The bartender produced a silver dustpan, small enough to be a child's toy, and swept up the pieces in one soundless, graceful motion. Dorothy discovered she'd half risen from her seat in reaction to the breaking glass. She sat down quickly, hoping no one had seen. There were servants to pick things up here. "No one breaks *my* Waterford!" her mother's voice rang in her mind's ear. At home, when her father's friends came in for a "quick one," they just drank out of the Li'l Abner jelly glasses, or whatever happened to be lying around. They poured their own drinks too. We don't *need* to have servants! Dorothy told herself proudly. But there was envy on the rim of her feelings, as surely as there were blood-red edges on the Virginia creeper leaves.

"Dorothy!" called Mrs. Hoade from somewhere, and Dorothy's agreeable shell of quiet observation broke, giving way to a sense of caution. Dorothy wanted very much to appear at ease. To say the right thing. She had not seen Mrs. Hoade since Mrs. Hoade had left her and the girls in the two rambling bedrooms that were to be theirs for the summer. She had first led them into the kitchen, stranding them there for the moment, and had taken the back stairs like a jackrabbit, saying something about being late for her own party. Dorothy had not dared follow her immediately, for fear Mrs. Hoade might have forgotten something and decided to come barreling downstairs at the same rate, crashing into all three of them. However, Mrs. Hoade had reappeared, more sedately, in a slip, remembering indeed that she'd forgotten to show Dorothy and the girls their rooms.

"Dear, you've met John, I see," she said. "Are you hungry? We'll get you something to eat." Mrs. Hoade's arm rested easily around Dorothy's shoulders. She had transformed herself somewhat from that afternoon's dowdiness, with tiny diamond earrings, a chunky diamond necklace, and a saffron yellow watered-silk dress. The whole effect was to make her look broader and squarer than before, but the silk! Dorothy wanted to finger the soft gleaming silk. Twelve dollars and fifty cents a yard, she calculated silently. And the diamonds! "Oh, come this way, dear, there's someone I want you to meet," Mrs. Hoade said, apparently forgetting Dorothy's empty stomach. Mr. Hoade, another man who had a swarthy, foreign look about him, and a woman stood near the deep end of the pool. The woman was so thin, so exquisitely dressed and combed and made up, that Dorothy wanted to hate her, but she couldn't because the face was intelligent and had a lively grin. She was introduced as Vita Berensen, Mrs. Hoade's oldest and best friend. Dorothy didn't catch the man's name.

"Kebab," he repeated for her. "George Kebab."

"Vita's publisher," said Mrs. Hoade with unabashed admiration.

"Just editor, I'm afraid," said Mr. Kebab.

"Vita's a famous author," said Mrs. Hoade. "She's been on television."

Dorothy's mouth opened. "You have?" she asked.

"I'm afraid Maria exaggerates," said the lively smile. "I was on for three minutes at six o'clock in the morning and I'm really not a famous author, not a really famous one."

"What books have you written?" Dorothy asked. "I might have read . . ."

"I'm sure you haven't," said Vita with a laugh. "There's only one and it's only a cookbook."

"It's called *Cooking for the Great and Near-Great*," said Mrs. Hoade loyally. "It's a best seller. And it's wonderful. She even had help from Madame Chiang Kaishek."

"Madame Chiang Kaishek!" said Dorothy, finding herself openmouthed again.

Vita chuckled. "I met her years ago," she explained. "When I was married to my first husband. He was in Roosevelt's entourage at Yalta. She and I became friends, and well, when she wanted to do this cookbook, I was a free-lance writer and I said I'd help her." Vita nudged Mrs. Hoade playfully with her elbow. "If it weren't for that picture of Madame Chiang holding up a chicken on the dust jacket, it wouldn't have sold five copies," she said. Vita turned back to Dorothy. "So you can see"— she swallowed the rest of her drink in one swanlike movement—"I'm hardly a famous author!" Was she expecting Dorothy to agree or disagree?

"There's a good Chinese restaurant we go to sometimes," Dorothy answered. She was about to tell this woman that she never ordered chow mein or chop suey like the rest of her family, but had more adventurous tastes.

"It isn't Chinese food," said Vita. "It's all French. The Generalissimo has a Belgian cook for his Western visitors. His Chinese guests are never great or even near-great."

Dorothy wanted to ask how Mrs. Chiang managed to write a cookbook if she didn't do any cooking when Lisa, smiling coyly, came to her side carrying a plate loaded with carefully arranged delicacies. It must have taken considerable time to compose it. Jenny followed looking dour. "How sweet of you!" said Mrs. Hoade to her daughter, and as soon as Dorothy was ensconced in a chaise, plate on her knees, she and her companions turned away as if Dorothy no longer existed.

"Lobster salad," said Jenny in a bored voice.

"And this, these?" Dorothy asked.

"Crab turnovers. And that's a quiche Lorraine. And those are white asparagus. They come out of a can but they're supposed to be better. And that's hearts of palm. That comes out of a can too."

"Hearts of what?"

"Palm," said Jenny. "We hate that food. After to-night, though, you'll have to eat with us."

Dorothy marveled at each new taste. Lisa was busy cramming a piece of cake into her mouth at a great rate, and so for once was quiet. Lisa had not stopped asking questions since that afternoon, when Dorothy had very nearly thrown her out of her room.

Mrs. Hoade had shown Dorothy through the upstairs of the house, all the while getting undressed and then dressed as they walked around. When she'd brought Dorothy back to her own room where she'd first left her suitcase, she'd discovered the girls had gone through her things rather thoroughly. "We unpacked for you," said Lisa blandly to Dorothy's angry face.

Dorothy had asked both girls to please wait for her in their own rooms.

"What size bra do you wear? What's your last name?" Lisa had gone on.

"Thirty-four B and Coughlin and if you don't mind . . ." Dorothy had paused for breath.

"You better put on something nicer than that," Lisa

had said. "Everybody's really dressed up. I saw a dress in your suitcase," she had added with her head cocked to one side. Dorothy had flounced out of her skirt and blouse and into the cotton dress the moment she'd got Lisa and Jenny out of the room. She'd had to threaten Lisa with a spanking to do it.

Luckily she hadn't cried in front of the girls. She'd had to stand for a moment, grasping the corners of the dark oak dresser, "her" dresser, with the ram's head carved over the center of the mirror. She'd ground her teeth until the ache in the back of her throat had subsided and then come back all over again and spent itself in tears when she'd seen that her best dress was hopelessly wrinkled because it was pressed up against *Ivanhoe* and *Nicholas Nickelby* all day long.

"Don't eat so fast, you'll get hiccups," she said gently to Lisa, as Lisa stuffed an enormous bite of cake into her mouth.

Lisa rolled her eyes, swallowed the cake, and whined to her sister, "Who does she think she is? A jailer?"

"I hope you don't try and teach us manners," said Jenny. "We get enough of that garbage at school. This is supposed to be a vacation, for heaven's sakes." Dorothy did not like the *for heaven's sakes* one bit but she was determined to make a new start with the girls.

"I'm sorry," she said genuinely.

Behind her, Mrs. Hoade's voice was getting louder and louder. Dorothy had seen her accept at least three drinks from a tray that circulated in the hands of a large, yellow-haired maid. Mrs. Hoade was speaking to Vita and Mr. Kebab. Something about a book. Her own book? Mr. Hoade was not successful in changing the subject.

At last Mrs. Hoade turned around and asked Dorothy to take the girls up to the house for cake and milk and television.

"No!" they howled in unison.

Dorothy tried to sound cheerful. She tried to march off with them, hand in hand, like the Pied Piper. They paid her no attention.

"I'm kissing Daddy good night," said Lisa, and she threw her arms around her father's neck.

"What have you got all over you?" he demanded, pushing her away with a terrible look at Dorothy.

"Icing," said Lisa, and glanced at her hands. She withdrew from her father quietly. It was the first quiet thing Dorothy had seen her do all day. I'll try to be nice to her, poor thing, Dorothy vowed.

"What a pretty dress you have, Lisa," she said when Lisa had fallen, strangely obedient, into file next to her.

"It's awful," said Lisa.

"I hate mine too," said Jenny.

Dorothy laughed. "I guess I hated dresses when I was a little girl too," she said.

"I'm not a little girl," Lisa declared.

"Neither am I," said Jenny.

"Did you say you were fifteen?" Lisa asked.

"Yes," answered Dorothy, wondering if this incessant questioning was retribution for her lie.

"You look younger," said Lisa.

"Mom said you were seventeen," Jenny remarked matter-of-factly.

Dorothy searched her memory with a small sensation of panic. Surely she hadn't told Mrs. Hoade that much of a lie. Could she have done so and blocked it out? But Jenny continued, "Just so we'd think you were bigger and scarier, I guess.

"Mom's a big liar anyway," she went on. "She usually tells people things that will suit them, depending on who they are. For instance, she tells Daddy's Jewish friends she's Jewish even though she isn't, and she told our Spanish nurse in South America that she was Catholic, which she isn't."

Lisa looked at the gold cross that hung from a chain around Dorothy's neck. "You Catholic?" she asked.

"Yes," Dorothy answered, "but I don't think . . ."

"I thought so," Lisa went on. "We have a girl in our class, Patty Finzio, who has a cross like that. She's the only Italian we have. Did Mom tell you she was Catholic?"

"No," said Dorothy, "and what's more, I don't think . . ."

"I know you're fourteen!" Lisa began to sing.

Dorothy flushed. "And just what makes you so smart?" she asked.

"You know that little statue of Mary or whoever it is on your bureau? I looked underneath and it says Dorothy whatever your name is, October sixth, nineteen forty-one. That's fourteen."

"For your information," Dorothy sputtered, "that's the Virgin Mary, Mother of our Lord. And also for your information it isn't nice to go through other people's things. I'll have to tell your mother." She decided to lock her door from now on.

"I'll tell her you're fourteen," said Lisa, tossing the flower of a Queen Anne's lace at her sister.

"That's a copper beech," said Jenny suddenly, coming to a halt in the middle of the lawn.

"How do you know?" Dorothy asked, grateful for a change of topic.

"I got my merit badge in nature," said Jenny. "I have twenty-two. I'll show you my sash. That's a Japanese maple and those are buttonwoods with the bark falling off and those big ones around the house are elms." Dorothy's gaze followed Jenny's forefinger. Lisa, at the first mention of merit badges, had run up to the house. For this Dorothy was also grateful.

On either side of the copper beech stood two chrome fountains, their water falling in graceful arcs. Whether their forms were artistic or utilitarian Dorothy couldn't guess. Ringing each fountain was a bed of primroses. She was struck by the incongruity, the fountains putting her in mind of an ugly new statue in front of the Newburgh City Hall and the roses suggesting life an infinite time ago, before cars and televisions and children who talked back.

Dorothy and Jenny walked slowly to the house, both of them solemn, neither talking. Once Dorothy glanced back at the party. She half expected Fred Astaire to come dancing through it. This place! The circular driveway, the fat green grass and the whispering trees. What a curious mixture of penance and treat this summer looked to become. There was no denying that the girls would be the bane of her life for the next two months unless she found a way to control them. But the place and the people she'd seen tonight, they were something wonderful. Her own backyard in Newburgh with its two straggly locust trees and the clothesline would never be quite as bearable again.

She wondered what her mother would think of the Hoades and their friends. She could see her mother's full red mouth become a tight little line of disapproval. Her mother would dislike these people with their easy money and their easy talk and their peacock clothing. She wouldn't care a bit what they thought of her. Maureen would hate them, just the way Maureen hated anyone who had more money or more time or more looks than she. "Think they're better than us, do they?" Maureen would sniff. Well, let them! Dorothy felt a small surge of loathing herself, but the more she let it encompass her the more she knew it was for the us, not the them, that she felt it. The us meant people who counted every last penny, whose halls smelled of cabbage and whose back stairs smelled of diapers. The part of you that wants what the Hoades have, Dorothy told herself, is a lazy, greedy, ungrateful part. I have a loving family and that's the most important thing in the whole world. These people have spoiled kids and divorces. But couldn't I have both money and a loving family? "No," said Maureen primly in her ear. Dorothy's feet glided through the thick dewy grass. She didn't believe Maureen.

"You're falling asleep," said Lisa sharply, and indeed, Dorothy had dozed off on the window seat of the library in front of the television. It was completely dark outside now. The lights were no longer on at the pool. Only a faint glow came from a little cottage down at the end of a grassy drive.

"I want some more cake," said Jenny. "Dinna won't get it for us."

"Who's Dinna?" Dorothy asked.

"The maid. The cook. You saw her tonight with the tray. She was going to take care of us this summer but we got you instead. Anyhow she put the cake on top of the fridge and we can't reach it. You get us some."

"Will you go to bed nicely if I do?" asked Dorothy.

"Yeah," said Jenny.

"I don't want any," Lisa announced, "and I don't want to go to bed."

Dorothy decided to put off dealing with this. She got up and left the library, where the television set had been placed between two bookcases. The bookcases ran from floor to ceiling and were filled with leather-bound volumes. Imagine having a library! Dorothy thought as she made her way downstairs. It's like something out of a romantic novel! But then the whole place is sort of like *Jane Eyre* or *Wuthering Heights*. All it needs is a fog and a ghost.

The kitchen was outsized; like most of the rooms in

the house, it appeared to have been designed to accommodate a dozen people. There were two sinks made of a dull pitted metal, and another in the pantry around the corner. The black iron stove had three ovens and six burners. Standing beside it, stirring milk in a pot, was a stumpy little woman in a nurse's uniform. Her glasses were very thick and she wore her hair tightly pulled back and braided in a coil at the back of her head. She smiled when Dorothy said hello, but she didn't answer. Finally she said something that sounded like "Ya ya" when Dorothy introduced herself.

"Dorothy," said Dorothy pointing to herself. Again the nurse smiled silently and smoothed out the wrinkles in her uniform skirt. Then she drank the warm milk in a single gulp.

Mrs. Hoade's voice, just a little shrill, drifted in from the living room. This gave Dorothy an excuse to walk as purposefully as possible in that direction. Thinking to say good night, she turned around once, but the nurse was gone. Since there was an argument going on between Mr. and Mrs. Hoade in the living room, Dorothy retreated to a respectful distance in the hall. She was not, however, completely out of earshot. Mr. Hoade was calling Mrs. Hoade a damn fool. He said it three times in a row.

"John, perhaps it was foolish, but I didn't have a chance to think . . ."

"And you're going to have to go through with it. Live with it!" he shouted.

"How was I to know?"

"You could have asked, for one thing!"

"John, I was as surprised as you when she told me. Now I just can't fire her and that's that."

Dorothy's ears pricked. Fire her! What had she done? Mr. Hoade was calling his wife careless now. A careless damn fool was what he said. "You could have asked," he repeated.

"Oh," Mrs. Hoade countered. "I'm supposed to ask the whole history of her family, is that it? Just tell me how you would have gone about doing that without sounding rude." Mrs. Hoade's voice turned sarcastic. "What does your father do? What is your mother's favorite food? What are the names and exact ages of your brothers and sisters? Do you have a dog? What is your dog's name? Is that the kind of interview you expected me to conduct?"

Oh, God, thought Dorothy, what can this be about? There's only one thing it could be. She couldn't have possibly found out I lied about Arthur's and Daddy's jobs so it's got to be that I have no experience. Maybe *she* doesn't mind but *he* does and I don't blame him. *Why* didn't I tell Mrs. Hoade that Maureen and Kevin and Terrance were older than me in the first place? She would have hired me anyway because she doesn't seem to care and at least I wouldn't have told a half lie. Half lie indeed! she snorted to herself. It's a lie. A sin of omission. Please, dear God, don't let him fire me. I'll try the best I can with the girls. I really will. Dorothy attempted to hear more of the conversation, but Mrs. Hoade was weeping now, sobbing miserably. Mr. Hoade's voice rose sharply, to an angry shriek, so odd for a man's voice. "All your stupid, misguided idea in the first place!" he said. "Why can't you take care of your own children like any other woman? Tell me that! Just tell me that!"

"John, I've decided I'm going to do some writing this summer. I thought . . . I'd like to do a cookbook. Like Vita. But better."

"Oh, beautiful!" was the last thing Dorothy heard Mr. Hoade say. She sighed and waited for them to stop arguing about the cookbook. Their voices were lowered beyond her hearing now. Dorothy's eyes gradually lost their focus in a sapphire-colored lamp that illuminated a drop-leaf table beside her.

On the table was a pewter dish. In the dish was an envelope, which had already been slit open—a bill, she guessed, as it had a cellophane window. "Modern Gala, Caterers for All Occasions," she read. Dorothy wondered how much this party had cost the Hoades. Inside of a moment she knew. Seventy-five dollars and forty cents for food, plus a hundred dollars for liquor. Dorothy's eyes popped. She replaced the bill in the envelope. Underneath it was another bill. It had already been taken from its envelope and lay faceup in the dish. It was from Crestview. Dorothy glanced at it as if she were not glancing at it. "Hoade, Katherine," it said, and went on to list three indecipherable medical expenses plus something called dietary. The whole thing came to five hundred twelve dollars and that was for one month only. My God! Dorothy whispered, and dropped both bills into the exact positions in which she had found them. She felt awful for having looked. She crossed herself and apologized for having taken God's name in vain. Five hundred twelve dollars for an old lady's medical care was bad enough, but one hundred seventy-five dollars and forty cents for one party was something else. It's a *sin* to waste money like that she told herself stoutly. No, it isn't, replied another part of Dorothy. It would be just *lovely* to have that kind of money to waste.

"Good night, Mr. Hoade," she said as pleasantly as she could when he strode out of the living room and nearly bumped into her in the hall."

"What are you doing here?" he asked and without waiting for an answer opened the front door and, slamming it behind him, ran down the front steps to his car.

Dorothy coughed politely as she entered the living room. Mrs. Hoade sat with her legs tucked up beneath her on the window seat. She watched Mr. Hoade's car pull out of the driveway and dabbed at her eyes. "Never fall in love, dear," she said, and got up and poured herself a drink. "I hope Mr. Hoade wasn't rude to you," she added.

"Oh, no," said Dorothy.

"He really can be so nice," said Mrs. Hoade, sipping from an old-fashioned glass. "You must have a bad first impression. We never have fights. We love each other very much."

"Oh . . . of course," said Dorothy.

"It's so funny," Mrs. Hoade said with a smile at the

ice in her drink. "It really was one of those love-at-first-sight things with me and John. I was very bad. Sit down, dear. Will you have a drink?"

"No, thank you," said Dorothy. She sat in a wing chair.

"What was I saying? Oh, yes. When I first met John. It was during the war. I'd gone to visit my best friend, Emily Baldwin. Emily and I had been friends all through school. She was engaged to a lovely boy. There was a dance on shipboard that night. This was in Norfolk, Virginia. The big naval base?"

"Yes," said Dorothy. She hoped this story would not take too long.

"At any rate, there was a dance. I hadn't come prepared, as I didn't know, and I had no dress. Well, I met John that morning when we visited Emily's fiancé. He asked me to the dance that night. I couldn't find a dress in Norfolk. Do you know what I did?"

"No," said Dorothy.

"Emily and I were the same size. That afternoon while we were waiting for the boys to get off duty, I got Emily drunk. I must have gotten three quarters of a bottle of vodka into her. I was drinking water, but she didn't know it. She was so sick she couldn't go to the dance. I borrowed her dress and went with John instead. Her fiancé, Richard, was killed at Midway three months later. Emily never saw him again. To this day she doesn't know I did it on purpose, but I'll never forgive myself. That's what love will do to you."

"Oh, dear" was all Dorothy could think to say. She

hated older peoples' stories about love. They were always so sappy. She thought she'd change the subject. "What a nifty house this is," she said, her eyes taking in the maroon damask drapes eagerly. An enormous Oriental rug, its pattern covered with birds and animals, covered the whole floor of the living room. The wood of the baby grand piano that stood in the corner seemed as soft as silk. The finish looked like honey in a jar. "What an elegant room," she added, guessing right then that nifty and elegant were a poor choice of words. "I just haven't ever been in a house like this, as big as this with all these things. . . ."

Mrs. Hoade chuckled. "I'm sure your house in Newburgh is lovely and homey," she said. "The humblest hearth if it is tended with love is worth all the palaces of the tsars, or is it kings? At any rate, the sentiment is the same."

"Oh, I know," said Dorothy earnestly. "It's just that you could fit three of my house into this one house!" She spread her arms to indicate the immensity she observed and knocked a small glass owl to the floor. Its ear broke off.

"It's all right!" said Mrs. Hoade, rushing over to pick up the owl.

"I'll pay for it!" said Dorothy. "Oh, my goodness. I'm so sorry. I'm so clumsy. I'll pay for it, Mrs. Hoade. I promise!" Dorothy discovered she had begun to cry.

"Please," said Mrs. Hoade. "It's only a doodad. You couldn't possibly pay for it anyway," she said with a laugh. "It's Steuben glass. Over twelve hundred dollars.

Now you couldn't do that, so let's just call it an accident. Dinna shouldn't have put it so near the edge of the table when she dusted, anyway."

"I'll pay for it, Mrs. Hoade. I'll pay for it anyway. My mother would make me," Dorothy gasped.

"Now listen," Mrs. Hoade broke in. She was still kneeling on the floor next to Dorothy. She put the owl and the ear on the table, and pulled Dorothy's trembling hand away from Dorothy's mouth. "Now listen to me, Dorothy." Mrs. Hoade said evenly. "It would take you three summers of work to pay for one silly piece of glass. Now I know exactly how you feel. I *sympathize*. Do you think I always had this kind of money? Believe me, I didn't. Now listen to this carefully because it's very important."

"Okay," said Dorothy shakily.

"I *hated* that owl. Here's a Kleenex. I certainly would never spend twelve hundred dollars on an owl. I even hate *real* owls. Now come. We'll change the subject. I'll show you some lovely pictures."

"All right," Dorothy agreed.

Mrs. Hoade pointed to a photograph on one of the tables. "That's how the house and grounds used to look," she said, "years ago before the stable was torn down. There used to be a stable and a greenhouse, and God knows why they tore them down. Fire hazards, I guess. Too much to keep up. See the stable at the back of that picture?"

"What are those?" Dorothy asked, picking up the photograph.

"Oh. Fishponds. They were filled in too. The fountains were put up recently." Dorothy thought she preferred the place as it had been before. A stable! She would have loved to have ridden a horse. The little cupids that held two jugs aloft in the middle of the fishponds certainly looked nicer than the chrome fountains. They went perfectly with the primroses, too.

"That was my father," said Mrs. Hoade, picking up another framed photograph.

"Who is that?" Dorothy asked, noticing a portrait of a woman, done in oils, hanging over a silver liquor tray at the bottom of the stairs.

"That's Lisa's and Jenny's great-grandmother—of course, when she was young," said Mrs. Hoade.

"People really dressed that way!" said Dorothy. "Look at that gorgeous dress!"

"Very impractical, if you ask me." Mrs. Hoade used a snippy tone that reminded Dorothy of Maureen.

Dorothy tried to remember the name of the painter whose style had been adopted for the portrait. Sister Elizabeth wanted her students to know about painters and styles. Gainsborough, that was it. The woman looked positively regal in her long flowing dress. There was something there that brought to mind Mother Superior. Certainly it wasn't the scarlet dress, not the eyes, for they were blue instead of brown and open, not hooded like Reverend Mother's, not the fine bones in the face, for they certainly held no false teeth. One hand was placed delicately on the head of a sitting greyhound, the other, at shoulder level, was poised on top of a stone column that still stood in the garden outside. Dorothy recognized it. She'd almost smacked into it and bumped her nose exactly on the spot where the long, supple fingers had relaxed for the painter on a long-gone afternoon.

One thing was certain. Mrs. Hoade did not much like the woman, but then people always had trouble with in-laws. Dorothy guessed that she must be Mr. Hoade's father's mother, since the name on the Crestview bill was Hoade too. Mrs. Hoade replaced the photograph of her father. "His plane was hit at Pearl Harbor," she said sadly.

I like her, Dorothy decided, as Mrs. Hoade drew an album of Jenny's and Lisa's baby pictures from a drawer in a huge mahogany table. She tried to think why. Was it because Mrs. Hoade seemed to need taking care of more even than her two daughters? A little. And also because she's sort of like an older me, Dorothy thought to her own surprise. Perhaps Mrs. Hoade had had a difficult time with Mr. Hoade's family. Dorothy wondered if the old lady in the picture had been mean. "Nobodies," that's what rich old families called people of the working class, very often. One day, Dorothy told herself for the fortieth time since having to slog through *The Forsyte Saga*, I'm going to write a best-selling book. I'll use an old matriarch as uppity as the one in that picture. I'll use a wife who works her way up from the slums and then marries a rich creep like Mr. Hoade. The family won't accept her, of course, but somehow she'll show them all.

The plot of Dorothy's book changed drastically every time she considered writing it, although the title remained constant. The best part about it was picturing Sister Elizabeth's face when the Book-of-the-Month Club sent her a copy of *Descent into Ashes*, by Dorothy Coughlin.

Dorothy tried to concentrate on the baby pictures. Most of them had been taken in Buenos Aires. "We lived here in Llewellyn," Mrs. Hoade explained, "until just before Lisa was born. She was born down there. I never want to do *that* again. South American hospitals . . ." She didn't explain further. "We'd better get them to bed," said Mrs. Hoade.

The best cure for insomnia, Dorothy had read in a mystery story, was to pretend you were an FBI agent assigned to watch a doorway for the emergence of a suspect. This apparently is very boring work. If you make yourself keep both eyes open, you'll surely enough begin to close one and then both and then bang! You're asleep. Dorothy fell into an exasperatingly wakeful state in her unfamiliar bed. Jenny and Lisa kept bounding out of the doorway she'd pictured and she couldn't get them back inside. Why do children do this to me? Why do they always get under my skin? she asked herself. The darkness of her room held no answer. You must try, she instructed herself. If you don't . . . If I don't, what? I'll be fired, of course, and have to go home in disgrace, without my money, have to spend the summer with Maureen. . . . More than that, though, she thought.

There is something in this place, in this house, with these people that I . . . that I want, or want to learn about. The key is the girls. If I'm able to manage them and last out the summer, then maybe . . . What would it be? There had been hints dropped that evening about some connection with Mr. Hoade and politics, with Mrs. Hoade and books. Books actually written by live people. Dorothy had never known anyone who had even met a writer, much less written a book themselves. There had been mention, too, of horseback riding. That was something she'd always wanted to do. So I'll try, she resolved. I'll do anything so that I don't have to— She pictured Maureen. Maureen, who'd married a high-school boyfriend and slipped away to a tiny rented house near the railway. She, Dorothy, never wanted to do that. Never wanted to buy cheap, ugly furniture on time. Never wanted to walk six blocks with a baby carriage and a wrinkled shopping bag to take advantage of a supermarket special on margarine. Just as Dorothy fell asleep, Reverend Mother's face appeared to her. "The wicked man fleeth where no man pursueth," said the unsmiling lips: "but the just, bold as a lion, shall be without dread."

"I won't do it the way Mrs. Hoade did," Dorothy murmured. "I won't marry some rich guy and have it fall in my lap. I'll work for it. I promise," she promised no one in particular.

Chapter

Three

"Jenny, won't you go in, just a little?" Dorothy pleaded.

"No. It's too cold."

"Jenny, it's been two weeks almost and you've hardly gotten wet up to your knees. It isn't cold. Not a bit. Your mom and dad made me promise I'd teach you to swim. Won't you try, Jenny?"

"No," said the grim little mouth, half hidden by the Turkish towel Jenny was chewing.

"Lisa, tell Jenny it isn't cold. You've been splashing around all morning. It's lovely! It's warm!"

"It's freezing," said Lisa.

Dorothy tried to sound cheerful. She tried to look as

if she and Lisa were in on a joke. "Oh, it is *not*!" she said
with a laugh. "If I do my double flip again will you just
get your feet wet?"

Jenny shrugged. "Maybe," she answered, still chewing her towel.

"Make it a cannonball dive and splash Matthew!" Lisa
instructed. Matthew, the gardener, knelt only a few feet
from the pool, weeding among the phlox and marigolds.
Matthew was deaf and dumb. Over the previous two
weeks Lisa had devised several tests to see if he really
was unable to hear or speak. Matthew did not flinch at
this latest test. Dorothy sprung off the diving board in
the best back flip she could manage.

As her head passed cleanly into the water, she smiled,
for she had not splashed him in the least. At the moment,
she almost envied the old man. How nice it would be
not to have to listen to Jenny and Lisa for a while. Dorothy bobbed up in the middle of the pool just in time to
see Lisa jump into the deep end of the pool. Her cannonball was not sufficient to get Matthew. Without turning
to watch her, he had disappeared just a second earlier
around the back of the arch.

"Damn!" said Lisa.

"Okay," Dorothy said when Lisa had dog-paddled to
the edge of the pool. "I've had enough. You do not go
into the deep end until you learn to swim better. Your
mother doesn't want you to dive. You try not to splash
people and you don't swear. All right, Lisa?"

"Get out of my life!" Lisa spluttered.

"If you do anything like that again, especially being

unkind to a poor deaf man, I'm going to spank you."

"You *can't* spank me. Mom *says* you can't."

"I'm warning you that I will."

"I dare you!" sang Lisa, beginning to dance on the rim of the pool.

Dorothy sat down in the nearest chaise longue. Keep your temper, she told herself. Remember she's only nine. Remember your mother's last letter. "Be patient and firm. Give them love and discipline and it will work out, I'm sure, dear. They will blossom before your eyes," said the gentle, clear handwriting, in the letter Dorothy used as a bookmark for *David Copperfield*. Her mother, of course, was three thousand miles away. And she's never seen kids like these, Dorothy thought to herself. She picked up her book and ran her hand over the blue airmail paper, as if to derive some strength from it. She watched Lisa flick tiny drops of water on her sister's shoulders. Jenny sat in a disconsolate lump, her feet dangling into the pool.

"Stop it. Cut it out," Jenny cried.

"Cut what out?"

"Cut out splashing me."

"Lisa, get the ball and we'll play some more volleyball in the pool," said Dorothy wearily. It was better to distract than punish, her mother's letter had advised.

"Scaredy-cat won't go in," Lisa whispered loudly.

"Lisa, just shut up," said Dorothy.

"You're not allowed to say that. I'm telling Mom!"

"Yes," Jenny agreed, "just shut your mouth, Miss Wet-Bed!"

Lisa shoved her sister right into the pool. Luckily Jenny had not been sitting too near the shallow end. She did not crack her head on the tiles. She only screamed and swallowed a great deal of water. By the time Dorothy had fished her out of the pool, dried her off, and calmed her wailing, Lisa had disappeared into the pool house.

"If you don't come out of there this instant," said Dorothy, blinking into the cavernous darkness of the pool house, "I'm coming in after you." No answer. Dorothy flicked the light switch. It did not work.

"It doesn't work," sobbed Jenny.

The pool house was filled with old gardening equipment, parts of the torn-down greenhouse, parts of a croquet set, a badminton set, and various other games that Dorothy could just make out, leaning against the walls, strewn over lawn mowers and piles of flower pots.

"The longer you stay, Lisa, the worse you're going to get it," said Dorothy.

"She won't come out," Jenny said. "Let's play Monopoly."

I hope she stays there for hours, Dorothy grumbled under her breath. Jenny, after all, wasn't so bad. She was a curious, quiet little girl, given at times to sitting in her "cave," a spacious, wicker-fronted closet in her parents' bathroom. There she kept her books and counted the money in her piggy bank almost every day. Dorothy had promised not to tell Lisa about the cave or the piggy bank.

"Love and discipline" indeed, Dorothy thought as she

sorted the money and the property cards. "Patient and firm" indeed. Dorothy glanced over at the pool house. In there was someone who was never going to change, at least not because of anything she, Dorothy, did or didn't do. Dorothy longed for some company other than the girls and Mrs. Hoade. Matthew might have been someone to talk to, if he could hear, which, of course, he couldn't. Dorothy liked the old man's rugged features and quiet ways. Given a beard he would have been a dead ringer for Abraham Lincoln, he was so tall and wraithlike. He looked wise, too. Someone to sit and listen to some sense from. But of course that wasn't possible. Miss Borg might have some good advice on the subject of children —after all, she was a baby nurse—but Miss Borg spoke no English and understood none. Nice Miss Borg. Sweet Miss Borg with the clear gray eyes and scrubbed pink cheeks. Dorothy and Miss Borg had become acquainted, after a fashion.

Several times, when Mrs. Hoade went to "check on the little one," as she put it, or on weekends when Mr. Hoade went down there, Dorothy had seen Miss Borg emerge from the cottage down the way and walk into a neighboring field to pick wild flowers. Dorothy had parked the girls in front of the television, from which they never moved in the evenings, and had followed the floating white uniform out into the meadow full of sweet peas and cornflowers and black-eyed Susans. These few minutes on occasional evenings had been pleasant, and although she could only smile and help Miss Borg carry her flowers, she felt for the short time that a headache had stopped awhile, that a noise had ceased. "Whatever language the woman speaks, Dorothy," Sister Elizabeth goaded in Dorothy's mind, "learn it! Learn it and give her your own God-given English in return." Dorothy had learned to say "*Guten Abend*" and with the help of Miss Borg's small German dictionary had tackled the names of a few flowers and weeds, which she promptly forgot. However, *Guten Abend*, good evening, was an improvement upon *Achtung!*, the only word of German she'd known before. Dorothy hoped that her company gave Miss Borg some satisfaction, but she couldn't read into the sad gray eyes, and the smile lines around the old woman's mouth seemed to belong to a once-happier person.

"Lisa, come out of there. Now!" Dorothy shouted.

"She won't," said Jenny. "Your turn."

"I better get her."

"Oh, leave her alone and let her cool off. It serves her right."

Dorothy sighed. "Never let the girls out of your sight." Those were Mrs. Hoade's instructions. "The place is full of rusty nails, old foundations, and other things I don't want them to get into, particularly Lisa, since she is allergic to tetanus shots and very impressionable. There are snakes down by the pond, rotting timbers near the baby's cottage. I want them in sight at all times."

"I promised your mother to keep you in sight all the time," Dorothy said.

"Well, she can't go far in that place. Let her stew. Do you want to buy Virginia Avenue?"

Jenny held her money fanned out like a bridge hand rather than in denominatory piles, as everyone else who played Monopoly always did. She also had extraordinary luck, and after making several advantageous deals with Dorothy managed to accumulate most of the important properties on the board. "What was Mom so happy about at lunch that she brought out wine?" Jenny asked.

"Oh, her book, I guess. It's going well. I guess it's fun doing all that cooking."

"With Dinna to clean up," said Jenny.

Dorothy laughed. Jenny was a perceptive one. "I think it's exciting. She's asked me to help her with her index cards at night. Community Chest. You inherit a hundred dollars."

"You like that?"

"I don't mind."

"Ecch," said Jenny. "I bet you're thinking your name will go on the book somewhere."

"I wasn't thinking that at all," said Dorothy. Jenny was too smart for her own good. Dorothy had hoped secretly not only that her name would be at least acknowledged in print, but that she might get to visit a television studio if Mrs. Hoade were to be on television once the book was published. From there Dorothy had hardly dared think, except . . . "I enjoy helping your mother. I'm good in English and we have to know how to organize notes for school and everything, so it's not hard," she said. "The other thing your mother was happy about was something to do with your father. Some new thing that might happen? Your turn."

"N?"

"That was it. What does N stand for?"

"That's a campaign of some kind. Move your piece back three spaces."

"Is your father in politics? There was a senator here last Friday night at the party but I . . ."

"Shake dice and pay owner four times the amount shown. No, he works for a drug company. At least he did. Now he does something called public relations. They've been talking about this for weeks. N probably stands for No-Drip or New Armpit. But it could be anything. Forty-four dollars, please. Thank you. You know what Dad did all that time in South America?"

"No, what?"

"He sold zillions of tubes of that stuff that sticks false teeth to the roof of your mouth to the South Americans. It was all rigged. Our government passed some kind of foreign-aid bill. When the South Americans got the money, one of the things they did was pass out thousands of sets of false teeth to all the beggars and peasants and things. Then Dad's company got into the act and sold all the false-teeth owners Suradent. My Dad's company wanted that foreign-aid bill badly. They even sent cases of Scotch to all the senators who voted for it. Saint Charles Place with two houses. A hundred and fifty, please."

"Jenny, you're making that up! Two hundred dollars for passing Go. You're making that up!"

"I'm not," said Jenny. "It's perfectly true. I always find out the facts. Just like Sergeant Friday."

"But that's against the law. Look at that nice senator your parents had here last weekend. Don't tell me he knows about that!"

"Him? You mean Rogers?"

"Yes."

"He's only in the state legislature. No, but you gotta believe me, Dorothy. You know one of my Dad's best friends, his golfing partner or whatever they call them, down in Buenos Aires, he had the account for Coke. He and Dad used to laugh because the more Coke this guy's company would sell, the more false teeth people would need and the more Suradent Dad would sell."

"They laughed about that? Go to Jail. Do not pass Go. Do not collect . . . They laughed about that?"

"Oh, yeah. Get Out of Jail Free card."

"People never really say what they mean. Like for instance, Mother. She wants us to think that kid out there has a cold. I bet you anything it's one of those what-do-you-call-its."

"Why do you think that?"

"Because she doesn't want Lisa to see it. She's afraid Lisa will have nightmares for a year. Why doesn't she just tell us? We don't want to see it anyway. Especially me. I hate all babies. Do you want to buy the Reading Railroad?"

Dorothy bit down on her lower lip. She thought how impressed she'd been to meet a person who actually was in the government. Jenny, who was only a kid, was not only unimpressed by a man who'd run for office, whose name had been in the paper, Jenny was positively blasé about a whole bunch of senators in Washington. "What's the matter? You look sad," Jenny asked.

"Nothing."

"Is it really one of those, you know . . . Did Mom tell you?"

"Yes, she did."

"Is it?"

"It's called a mongoloid."

"Do you want to buy that railroad? See?"

"See what?"

"See, I was right. I'm glad they keep it out there. I don't want any stinky crying babies around the house."

Dorothy laughed. She spent her last two hundred dollars on the Reading Railroad and promptly landed on Jenny's Boardwalk hotel. "That's the end of the game, Jenny. I can't pay." She began sorting the money out again. "I guess I don't care for babies so much either. I guess that's an awful thing to admit."

"Do you have babies at your house?"

"No. My sister has one, though. A girl. I mean she's a really cute baby. Everyone says so and my sister loves her and all, but I don't see how anyone can stand going goo-goo, ga-ga all day without going out of their minds. Besides, most of the time babies smell awful, unless they've just been washed, and then before you know it they smell hideous again. I don't know. I suppose it would be good for me to learn to like them since I'll probably have to have them someday."

"Not me," said Jenny stretching out like a contented cat on the warm, sun-speckled tiles. "Not me, oh, boy."

Dorothy had almost forgotten about Lisa. She lay back on the comfortable cushions of her deck lounge and played with a wild grape vine that hung from a trellis overhead. She thought of Maureen. Maureen wheeling the baby carriage with its crinoline fly netting and its tremendous springs that were better by far than the springs in Maureen's and Arthur's Chevy. She began to picture Maureen's dumpy little house on Seale Street. Practically all the girls in Maureen's class in high school who had not gone on to college or become nuns had babies now. There had been wedding showers and then weddings and then baby showers. The minute Terrance graduated from Holy Cross, he said, he was going to marry Angela, his steady. He and Angela would probably have a baby soon after, too. They would move into an apartment with ugly old furniture that never wore out, or ugly new furniture that fell apart in a year. Once, when Maureen had been down with the flu, Dorothy had wheeled Bridget's carriage up the sleepy Wednesday-afternoon street. A street she knew to be inhabited at that hour only by housewives and children. She'd felt like an invalid herself. "This is the loveliest place in the world," she found herself saying to Jenny.

"It's nice," Jenny agreed. "I don't really remember it from before. I was too little. I don't think Lisa was even born then. Mom's talked about coming back here before but she's never yet had the courage to leave Daddy. She was trying to get him to spend more than two nights a week here but he's too busy in the city. She's been away from him all during the time she was . . . pregnant. I hate that word. She was down here and he was mostly in Buenos Aires and we had to go to boarding school. I hate boarding school. Anyway, if you ever catch Mom crying it's because she misses Daddy. Are you poor?"

"What?" asked Dorothy.

"Are you from a poor family? Does your father have to have a job in a factory and everything?"

"My father's a policeman," said Dorothy. "He certainly doesn't work in a factory and we certainly are not poor."

"There's nothing wrong with poorness," said Jenny.

"Poverty," Dorothy corrected.

"My daddy wastes money," Jenny went on conspiratorially. "Least Mom says he does. He goes to Las Vegas and he's always talking about making more money. I hear through their door. Once he told her he needed her love and support and she said she tried to be a good wife but he was asking too much and gonna ruin everything. Lisa heard that too. Mom was crying. That made Lisa cry and she got sick and I had to sleep with her in bed all night so she wouldn't cry. So she shouldn't push me into pools, I'll say."

"Jenny, you shouldn't tell people about your parents like that. It isn't respectful."

"You wanna know what Mom said once to Daddy about the money that . . ."

A shadow fell over the top of the Monopoly box. "Hi!" said a voice.

Dorothy looked up, squinting in the afternoon sun. "Yes?" she said, rising to her feet.

"I'm Carol Baldinger. You can call me Baldy." A nice solid hand was extended. Dorothy shook it. Its owner looked to be not much older than she. Baldy was chunky and muscular, and very curly-haired. She was not pretty. She wore horn-rimmed glasses and smiled a very big smile.

"I'm Dorothy Coughlin and this is Jenny," said Dorothy, wondering suddenly if this person had been asked to replace her because she'd done so badly with the girls that Mrs. Hoade had given up. "You're not . . . going to take care of the girls, are you?" Dorothy asked.

"No. I answered an ad for riding instructor. I'm to drive the girls to the stable starting next week. You can come too. Mrs. Hoag said it would be okay. I came down to say hello," said Baldy.

"Well, hello," said Dorothy, noticing at that moment the beautifully cut riding pants and the soft brown leather boots on Baldy's feet. They were not cowboy boots. They were something much much nicer. "It's Hoade, by the way, not Hoag," she added.

"Oh. I'm so bad at names. I don't know anyone here, much. My uncle's away buying stock in France and Ireland. I'm taking care of his stable. It's just a few miles away. I'm glad there'll be someone around to talk to," Baldy said with another big smile. "It's lonely here."

"Stock?" asked Dorothy.

"Horses. Race horses. He goes every summer. Where's the other little girl? I thought there were two."

"She just ran out," Jenny said calmly. "While you were talking."

THREE

"Lisa!" Dorothy yelled. No answer. "Please watch Jenny for a sec? Please, would you?" she asked Baldy, and without waiting for her reply, she charged off across the lawn.

She didn't want to call too loudly for fear of Mrs. Hoade overhearing. Mrs. Hoade was busy with Dinna on one of the interminable "secret" recipes, known only to Dinna and her Pennsylvania Dutch family, that was going to be in *Pennsylvania Surprise!*, which was the title of Mrs. Hoade's book.

There was no Lisa to be seen, either darting among the trees or running anywhere across the lawn. The grounds of the house and the woods beyond looked larger to Dorothy than they ever had before. Dorothy ran down toward the overgrown drive that led to the pond on one side and the cottage on the other.

"Lisa! Lisa!" she yelled, now that she was out of range of the big house. No answer came from the surrounding brambles, scrubby oaks, and pine trees that lined the path.

Dorothy discovered she was annoyed at Lisa for running away and just as much annoyed at Mrs. Hoade for making such an issue of watching the girls every minute. After all, when she, Dorothy, had been younger even than Lisa, she had been allowed to walk to and from school alone. There were certainly more dangers on Newburgh, New York, streets than on this quiet estate.

On Dorothy's right, a short walk through leg-searing grasses, was a pond. It seemed stagnant and didn't appear to be deep. Lisa had told her a monster lived in it, just like the Loch Ness monster. Dorothy stared, out of breath now. The muddy green surface answered no shouts. "Lisa!" she called to the trees. There were so many places for a child to hide here. Matthew was not around. He wouldn't have noticed Lisa anyway. Perhaps Miss Borg had seen her. Perhaps Dorothy could convey her question without too much trouble. It was worth a try.

She stamped back through the brambles and poison ivy until she reached the grassy path again. Dorothy guessed Miss Borg might ask her in for a cup of tea. Nice, grandmotherly persons always did that. It was too bad she hadn't time for it. She would have liked some of Miss Borg's quiet company. Better not to, anyway. Had Mrs. Hoade told her not to go to the cottage or was it just the girls who were not supposed to go? Dorothy, for reasons she hadn't puzzled out, had not told Mrs. Hoade about her walks with Miss Borg.

The little house itself was certainly different from the main building. Dorothy could tell easily that it was fairly new and a cheap building at that. Instead of clapboard, it was built of inexpensive siding meant to look like clapboard, same as in all the developments around Maureen's neighborhood. The roof was done out of unpleasant purplish shingle, so much in contrast to the curved red and brown tiles on the roof of the big house. She knocked a little timidly on the door.

A chair scraped against the floor. Miss Borg's pink

face appeared between the curtains of the window for a moment. The door opened, allowing the odor of something that reminded Dorothy of a Salvation Army store or her great-aunt Ruth's parlor to emerge. Miss Borg shut the door firmly behind her and said, "*Was?*"

"I'm sorry to bother you," Dorothy said, sensing that indeed she had bothered Miss Borg. "Have you seen Lisa? Lisa? The little girl, Lisa?" she asked very slowly, amplifying her words with gestures for see and little.

"*Was?*" asked Miss Borg again in a no more obliging tone. Dorothy shook her head. Miss Borg's word sounded like *Vuss*. It probably meant What-are-you-trying-to-say-you-idiot? "How's the baby?" Dorothy asked conversationally.

Miss Borg looked sharply at Dorothy's broad, innocent smile and empty, cradling arms.

"*Sie ist in ihrem Bad*," said the nurse and immediately went back into the house, closing the door with a firm click. Dorothy stared stupidly for a minute at the closed door. I guess it's just not my day, she thought. When is it going to be my day? She turned and walked back up the path. When I collect my four hundred George Washingtons on Labor Day. That's when.

"Dorothy," said Mrs. Hoade. "I would like a word with you." Dorothy sat down in the nearest chair, a straight-backed one in the hall. She folded her hands, swallowed hard, and looked up as sincerely as she could. If she hadn't known she was going to be severely reprimanded she would have had a difficult time not laughing, for Mrs. Hoade was covered with much more than the usual amount of flour that coated her apron and clothing after one of her sessions in the kitchen with Dinna. This time there was flour in Mrs. Hoade's hair, and she had evidently dropped an egg on or in her shoe. Her right hand had fought another unsuccessful battle with yet another leaky Esterbrook fountain pen.

"I hardly know where to begin," Mrs. Hoade began.

"I'm very sorry, Mrs. Hoade," Dorothy began.

"Lisa, by the way, is upstairs or was upstairs watching *Frankenstein* on television. I understand she was out of your sight, that you had no idea where she was for over an hour while you played Monopoly with Jenny. Is that true?"

"Yes, Mrs. Hoade. Well, sort of. She was in the pool house."

"Where she could have hurt herself on numerous rusty objects."

"I guess so, Mrs. Hoade."

"And you disturbed Miss Borg, I understand? And went down where I specifically told you not to go?"

"But . . ."

"That area is full of old foundations and rotting wood. There are black widow spiders and holes in the ground. If you injured yourself, your clever lawyer brother could sue us. Not that he would, but he could. You are not to go there again."

"Yes, Mrs. Hoade."

"And you are not to let Lisa watch horror movies or any television during the day. Her . . . little problem at night has cleared up in the past two weeks, and if it starts again I will have only you to blame, Dorothy, for threatening her with spankings, for using words like shut up, and for virtually imprisoning her in a dark, dangerous place like the pool house."

"But . . ."

"Is that clear?"

"Yes, Mrs. Hoade, but . . ."

"Now for the worst thing," Mrs. Hoade rubbed her floury nose with the back of her inky hand. "What you said to Jenny."

"What did I say to Jenny?"

"About the baby. I'm sure you heard me, the very first day you were here. In the car, as a matter of fact. *We are saying the baby has a cold.*"

"But . . ."

"Jenny has already told Lisa what you said and Lisa has come to me and complained about a monster being down there. A monster!"

"Mrs. Hoade, that's the monster in the pond. She . . ."

"No, Dorothy. A girl in Lisa's class had the misfortune of having a baby brother who . . . who was physically . . . who was not at all normal. Now both girls are convinced their sister is, in Lisa's words, a freak. I won't go into detail."

"But it isn't true about the cold and Jenny knew it anyway and I couldn't lie to her, Mrs. Hoade. I . . ."

"Because you are a Roman Catholic, perhaps?" asked Mrs. Hoade.

"No, but . . ."

"Does that cross around your neck give you a leg up on the rest of the world as far as truth is concerned?"

"No, but . . ."

"Have you ever told a lie? A lie that makes it easier for people? A lie that hurts no one?"

Dorothy nodded.

"Very well. By the way. When that girl, Carol Baldinger, came back here with Jenny, Jenny had been quite happily splashing all around the pool."

"Jenny?"

"Carol had jumped in with her, fully clothed. They had a wonderful time. Sometimes it's better to be child-like with children instead of showing them how good you are at diving and racing. Now. I have ten apple pies to complete and the pastry is melting. Please go upstairs and see that they haven't turned *Frankenstein* back on."

Dorothy climbed the creaky stairs slowly. She compressed her mouth. Roman Catholic indeed. Truth. What was the truth? The truth was that she might get fired. Baldy indeed. But supposing Mrs. Hoade hired someone like Baldy? A natural with children. Mrs. Hoade didn't seem so terrific with children, even her own kids. Look how she'd botched the whole business about a simple mongoloid baby. It was bad for Jenny and Lisa to have been lied to. They had found out anyway. And it was bad for the poor baby too. Mrs. Saxon, down at the end of the next block from Dorothy's house, had had one of those mongoloid babies. "Over my dead body," Mrs. Saxon had said to Dorothy's mother numerous times, "would we ever stash Chucky away like some people do." Mrs. Saxon always said this with a bit of relish in her voice and a glance over her shoulder as if the "some people" were right there in the living room. Hmmph! Dorothy said to herself. If Mrs. Hoade gets going again I'll just tell her what I think about keeping a little baby hidden in some gazebo . . . was gazebo the right word? It sounded sufficiently sinful, at any rate . . . hidden away from its own sisters. Why I could even report it to some interested party. It isn't *right!*

FAMILY SHAME EXPOSED! ran the headline in Dorothy's imagination.

> The Pennsylvania Society for the Prevention of Cruelty to Children today awarded its highest accolade to Dorothy Coughlin, a sophomore at Sacred Heart Academy in Newburgh, New York, for her courageous exposure of a mongoloid child, separated from its parents and sisters on an estate in Llewellyn. The child, daughter of wealthy advertising magnate John Hoade and his scatterbrained wife, Maria, has been placed in a foster home.
>
> The Society has offered to recompense Miss Coughlin for her lost salary, but Miss Coughlin has refused, saying that although she was fired from her job after calling this paper, her salary will be more than made up in speakers' fees. Her first address will be given to the assembled students and Sisters at Sacred Heart.

"You really got it, didn't you?" asked Lisa from the top of the stairs.

"Someday, Lisa, you're going to learn to mind your own business," Dorothy snapped. "What's on that television?"

Dorothy watched for a minute as Frankenstein teetered back and forth on the screen. She switched the channel to a cartoon program.

"I guess I got you into trouble, didn't I?" Jenny asked.

"I guess you did."

Jenny paused. "I didn't mean it," she said almost angrily.

"You're forgiven."

"Did you see it? Her?"

"Nope."

"How's that old nurse? What's she like?" Jenny went on in an easier tone.

"She doesn't speak English. She just said . . . what did she say to me? Something that sounded like *Zee iss innair baht.*

"I know what that means," Jenny began.

"Smarty," said Lisa, "I speak twice as good Spanish as you do. You do not know what that means."

"It isn't Spanish, Lisa," said Dorothy calmly. The cartoons jumped crazily around the screen in front of her. Dorothy turned to look out the window. Matthew was driving Dinna home. The gravel crunched in the driveway.

"It means . . ." Jenny screwed up her face in concentration. "It means she's in her bed . . . no, in her *bath*. That's what it means."

"Always have to be a know-it-all," Lisa broke in.

Dorothy closed her eyes. Maybe I'll just quit before I'm fired, she thought.

"Dorothy!" called Mrs. Hoade from the stairwell. "Doro*thy*!"

Dorothy got up and went to the head of the stairs. One more thing, she decided, if I've done one more thing wrong I'm just going to up and leave and go home to Maureen. "Yes, Mrs. Hoade?"

"Dorothy, do you know how to get an apple pie out of its pan once it's finished baking? Is it supposed to come out of the pan or stay in? Dinna's gone home." Mrs. Hoade sighed. "Would you please come help me take these dreadful pies out of these awful pans?"

Chapter

Four

"No, I don't want to!" Jenny clung to the fence rail. Dorothy held Texas's reins and watched Baldy carefully. How was Baldy the genius going to accomplish this?

"Jenny," said Baldy seriously, "you promised last week and the week before that you'd just sit in the saddle for one second. Now last week I let you get away with it. This week you have to do it. I promise. One second. No more."

"No."

"Trust me."

"Everyone says one second. What they mean is one hour."

"You know what?"

"What?" asked Jenny, her eyes beginning to brim with tears.

"This is a loaded water pistol, right?"

"Yeah?" asked Jenny guardedly.

"Okay. Now. If I put you in that saddle for more than one second, maybe two, 'cause you're heavy to lift, you can let me have it full in the face."

"You mean squirt you?"

"Is it a deal?"

"Okay."

Baldy lifted Jenny gently off the fence rail. "I'm counting!" Jenny shrieked.

"One and two and three!" said Baldy, and she placed Jenny exactly back where she'd been sitting after a second's pause in Texas's unmoving saddle. "Now. You know what you can do?"

"What?" asked Jenny looking at the pistol, which she hadn't been able to use.

"You can squirt me anyway! I'm hot as blazes!" Baldy lay back on the soft earth and opened her mouth. Jenny giggled. She pulled the trigger. Baldy screamed.

God! thought Dorothy. I could never do that. It just isn't in me to clown with kids. Jenny laughed, a nice solid child's laugh at an unexpected delight. Dorothy had never heard such a carefree sound from Jenny before. The stream of water poured directly into Baldy's open mouth, splashing her face a bit as she writhed on the ground. Pride, Dorothy reminded herself. I've always been told I'm so full of pride, and it's true. Too

proud to really play with kids. Too proud . . . Oh
had Maureen laid it on with a trowel last night! "Mom
says I'm supposed to call and check on you," she announced and then tried to pack the allotted three minutes
with questions about Dorothy's time off and whether
Dorothy could arrange to come home for a weekend.
Somehow Maureen had wangled the truth out of her
sister. "What do you mean she gives you a day off a
week? What are you doing with it in the middle of
nowhere? *Riding?* Riding horses? Two whole afternoons?"

Dorothy didn't want to think about the conversation.
She let Texas's bridle go, as Baldy had hold of it now.
Jenny had agreed to go around the back ring once,
provided she was out of sight of Dorothy and Lisa.
Dorothy got into Charley's saddle. Charley was "her"
bay gelding. She followed Lisa around the track in a
slow trot. "Heels down," she told Lisa. She'd learned a
lot from Baldy in two short weeks.

Maureen had gone on to say, "You are first of all
crazy. Second of all selfish and third of all proud!"

"Maureen," Dorothy had replied, trying to put some
understanding in her voice. "Maureen, please!"

"You're crazy because you could fall off one of those
animals and get killed or get paralyzed from the neck
down and be in a wheelchair for the rest of your life.
You're selfish, because you could save up your days and
give me a little help. And you're proud, because all these
rich people have turned your head. You'll never be able
to ride back home so what's the good of learning how?"

"It's just fun," Dorothy had explained.

"Are you doing your summer reading? How many books have you finished?"

Dorothy had explained that her evenings had mostly been spent helping Mrs. Hoade organize her cookbook. Maureen had observed that this too was crazy. "Too proud to do a little cooking at home but not too proud to get her name into a book, isn't that right?" Yes, that was right, but Dorothy hadn't admitted it to Maureen. "And what about Mass? Are you going to confession and Mass?" Maureen wanted to know.

"Maureen," Dorothy had answered, "three minutes are up."

"I'm expecting you Labor Day weekend. Arthur and I are making plans."

"I'll have to see how long Mrs. Hoade wants me to stay. I'll try."

"Labor Day weekend, Dorothy."

"Three minutes, Maureen!"

Dorothy posted up and down in Charley's saddle. She loved the sound of so many squeaking leather parts. "Dorothy?" Lisa asked.

"Yes?"

"Can I squirt you with a water pistol if you get too hot?"

"No," said Dorothy quickly.

Later that afternoon, when she and Baldy were exploring the countryside, on Charley and on Baldy's horse, Gabriel, Dorothy admitted she felt miserable about the girls. That they disliked her and with reason. "I wish

I had your humility and . . . and well, sense of humor," she said lamely. Baldy thought that was extremely funny because humility and sense of humor had gotten her no place at all.

Baldy was eighteen or maybe nineteen, Dorothy wasn't sure. She attended a junior college somewhere in New England, where, Baldy admitted, they didn't make her do much studying. She was majoring in riding—Equestrian Studies it was called. She had Gabriel stabled there all the school year. She'd been giving riding lessons ever since she could remember, she'd told Dorothy. Not because she needed money but because she loved being with kids. All kids, any kids. Even Jenny and Lisa. Her one ambition was to ride for the U.S. Olympic team. She'd already taken two firsts in the McClay medal class at the Madison Square Garden Horse Show. She would send Dorothy a ticket for next year's show, she said, and her parents would take them all out for dinner at Lüchow's afterward, where they always went after the National Horse Show.

Baldy's secret, Dorothy discovered very quickly, was that she could barely read at all. She could get through the instructions on a bottle of liniment all right, she could manage the comics and horse magazines, but books were impossible for her. Although the college she attended was quite lenient, all the more so because her father was a trustee, she was still expected to be somewhat educated. That was where Baldy needed Dorothy.

Mrs. Hoade didn't mind at all when Baldy came over to sit by the pool, a book tucked meekly under her arm.

Baldy and even the girls listened while Dorothy explained all the big words and fancy ideas in *Adventures in English Literature.* Neither did Mrs. Hoade mind Dorothy taking her weekly day off in halves. The girls during these afternoons were allowed to watch soap operas while their mother was down in the kitchen with Dinna.

"What I want to know, Baldy," Dorothy asked as they urged their horses to trot over a soft pine-needle-covered trail, "is whether you had that water pistol in mind before the lesson today?"

Baldy shooed a fly away from Gabriel's ears with her switch. "I keep it around the barn," she said with a smile. "It always works. I keep one at my parents' stable in Greenwich and up at school, 'cause I give lessons to faculty kids there. Jenny's not the first kid who's been afraid to get into a saddle."

"Somehow I just couldn't let anybody squirt me in the face. Especially a nasty little brat," said Dorothy sadly.

"They can't help it. It's always the parents' fault."

"I know. I can't stand their father. Mrs. Hoade is nice but she's got a lot on her mind. She's writing a book and she's worried about her baby. She goes down there evenings and lets me organize all her notes. You should see her notes."

"I couldn't organize notes for all the tea in China," said Baldy. "What's the matter with the baby?"

"Mongoloid."

"Oh."

"Drives him crazy. I think it also drives him crazy that he didn't have a son. You know these men from families that go back to the Mayflower? They always have to have juniors and George Finky Uppersnouts the Fourth . . ." Dorothy stopped herself. Baldy was shaking her finger in good humor.

"Isn't that true of every man? Rich or poor?" she asked.

"I guess so. But they always have a fight when he goes down to the cottage on weekends when he's home. Afterward they always have a fight. They turn up the record player very loud so the kids and I don't hear."

"I like George Finky Uppersnout the Fourth," said Baldy. "I have a cousin whose name is John Adams Baldinger Mellon the Third." She paused. "You know, I once taught a little boy, a retarded little boy everyone thought was useless, to ride. If you have a little patience with the girls they'll come around. They're already less obnoxious than they were."

"Thanks to you," said Dorothy. She wished she could find a way to tell Baldy just how much the summer had improved since their riding lessons had begun. The sessions "cracking books," as Dorothy put it, were pleasant and flattering as well. She had assured Baldy that she had only a freshman-in-high-school education, but Baldy had pronounced it to be better than anyone's at Butler Junior College. She loved to listen to Dorothy read "Stopping by Woods on a Snowy Evening" or "Miniver Cheevy." Even the girls now asked Dorothy to read them *Just So Stories* before bedtime. Baldy said she had

hope now of passing her next term, a requirement her father had laid down if she was to continue stabling Gabriel
at school. All Dorothy had to do was read Sister Elizabeth's favorite poetry in Sister Elizabeth's favorite dra-
matic voices and explain to Baldy Sister Elizabeth's
opinions of what was good and what was bad. She did
not mention Sister Elizabeth, however, and Baldy
thought Dorothy was a genius.

Horses were Baldy's favorite topic of discussion. She
said Dorothy was a "natural horsewoman" and she
flooded her ears with the facts of horse shows, training,
births, deaths, and ailments.

They came to a clearing in the woods and stopped
for a moment to look over the farms in the valley.

"Closest thing I've ever seen to English downs,"
Baldy said, patting Gabriel's sweating neck.

"Yes," said Dorothy, having no idea what an English
down looked like.

"Too bad about that tractor. What a racket it makes.
They should plow with horses," Baldy said, pointing to
a distant yellow tractor.

Again Dorothy agreed. She did not mention to Baldy
that farmers had to use tractors to make their farms
efficient. Certainly anyone who'd had a basic American
history course knew that. Most farmers had to struggle
to keep alive.

"If horses ruled the world, instead of people," Baldy
insisted with sudden vigor, "things would be a whole
lot better. We probably wouldn't have any wars."

"Probably not," said Dorothy. There was something

in Baldy's attitude about horses and tractors that had nothing to do with basic history courses. It had more to do with not realizing that people had to work to live. Dorothy felt a small shiver at the base of her spine.

"What's the matter?" Baldy asked suddenly.

Dorothy inhaled deeply. "Let's go," she said looking at the watch Mrs. Hoade had lent her. "We only have an hour. I have to get back by five. Mrs. Hoade's doing a bread recipe with Dinna. She wants to take my picture punching down the dough."

"Fine," said Baldy. "We're not really far from your place, as a matter of fact. I can drop you off and take Charley back on a lead line."

"No, I left my sweater at your stable."

"Okay, we'll go a new way. There's a graveyard I wanted to show you just up here, and a covered bridge. Tree-covered, that is." They began to trot again. "What's the matter?" Baldy repeated.

"Oh, nothing."

"Come on."

"Well, I was thinking about a party the Hoades had last weekend. I got to spend about an hour and a half at it. I was supposed to help Dinna serve, but I couldn't stand it so I talked to people. You know I told you, Baldy, that my dad was chief of police?"

"Yes?"

"Well, he isn't. He's just a . . . a cop with a beat. Do you know I come from a really poor family compared to you or the Hoades? All that stuff I told you about my family having a big old castle on the Irish sea is a lie. My grandfather was never a nobleman put to death by the English. My mother is not related to James Joyce and we don't live in Hyde Park, New York. We live in Newburgh. In case you haven't heard of it, it's a crummy little town on the Hudson River."

Baldy pulled Gabriel up short next to Dorothy. "Why did you tell me that . . . all that then?" she asked.

"I don't know," said Dorothy. She nudged Charley on and didn't look at Baldy. "I guess I just wanted to tell you it was all a pack of lies. I wish it were true, but none of it is." She ducked as a leafy branch nearly hit her in the face.

"Up here," said Baldy. "Go to your right."

Clear, limpid water, hardly stirring, formed a pool under a wooden bridge. Ancient weeping willows dangled their lower branches into it, the leaves mirrored perfectly in the late afternoon light. Other branches woven and twined around each other made an arch at the end of the bridge. Both girls had to lay their heads on their horses' necks, not to get swiped by it. "This always reminds me of *Black Beauty*, crossing this bridge," said Baldy. "It's probably the only book I ever finished."

"Oh, come on, Baldy," said Dorothy, feeling a little cheered again.

"Maybe *King of the Wind* and a Nancy Drew or two," Baldy amended. "Anyway, Black Beauty wouldn't cross a bridge because he knew it had rotten wood in it. Horses know all kinds of things," she added mysteriously.

"Horses have powers unknown to man. That's why I like them so much better than people. There's the graveyard I told you about. I've never had the nerve to stop. Shall we look?"

"Sure," Dorothy agreed. "It's a funny place for a graveyard and it's so tiny!"

"It's a private one, a family one. There's lots in this part of the country." Baldy dismounted. "Let's see what the names are."

Dorothy dismounted too. Baldy had to retie the knot in Charley's reins. "He'll get away if you tie it like that," she explained and showed Dorothy how to tether a horse. "What do the names say? How far do they go back?" she asked, taking off her horn-rims and polishing them on her shirt.

A whole family with a whole private graveyard all their own, Dorothy thought. Amazing. "Most of them say Coburg, one Miller here. Some are really old," Dorothy said, lifting a curtain of vines from an ancient stone cross. "Look at this! From the eighteenth century. Emma, wife of John, mother of Asa. No last name."

"It isn't creepy, is it?" Baldy asked. "I thought it would be."

"It should be," Dorothy answered. She looked up at the sun through the bright-green maple leaves of the surrounding woods. A cardinal called to its mate, and a rabbit showed its face around one of the stones. "But it isn't. I don't think anybody's been here in years."

"I'll show you two more next week," said Baldy. "It

sure is nice to have company riding. I'm all alone except for Kenny, the groom, and he never stops to look at anything."

Dorothy hoisted herself back up in the saddle. She looked again at the quiet graveyard and crossed herself. Then she noticed a stone that had carved on it the name Chin Wang. There was no date.

"Houseboy," said Baldy. "Chinese. People used to bury their servants if they'd been faithful, right with the rest of the family."

"Do you . . . does your family have a houseboy?" Dorothy asked in a small voice.

"No," Baldy answered. She laughed. "That's gone long ago. We just have a cook, Louise, and one maid and Julio, who doubles as gardener and chauffeur. My parents board our horses in Greenwich. That's how come I like to stay at Uncle's and really live on the stable grounds. Dorothy?"

"Yes?"

"How come you did that thing back there?"

"You mean crossing myself?"

"Yes."

"Graveyard. I don't know. Just in case."

"Does it help?"

"I guess so," she said, but she wondered about that. Perhaps, she decided, crossing myself would help if I had some dreadful disease and wanted God to cure me. And maybe it helps me not get run over by cars. And maybe, if I were standing under an avalanche and I crossed myself, a boulder would just miss me. But it doesn't seem to help at all when I'm trying to get out of my mind what's on my mind. Dorothy ran her fore-finger over the two little brass rivets at the top of her saddle. She just loved to listen to the leather, to pull the reins back and forth in her hands, adjusting them, to feel the stirrups hard against the heels of her loafers. She wished she had beautiful high-top boots like Baldy's. Those weren't even Baldy's good boots. What was on her mind was houseboys and cooks and the Pennsylvania countryside in the summer.

"You look sad again. Is it about . . ." Baldy licked her lips, evidently not knowing how to go on.

"You know something?" Dorothy broke in. "Do you know something funny? Before this summer I had never, except in a restaurant, eaten butter in my whole life? Even known what a filet-mignon steak was?"

"You've never eaten butter!"

"Margarine. My mother buys canned vegetables on special. We have franks and beans twice a week and cod-fish on Fridays."

"But why does that bother you so? Why are you so ashamed of that and the fact that your dad's a police-man?" Baldy asked desperately.

"Because . . . I don't know." Dorothy heard her voice tremble a little. "A few weeks ago Mrs. Hoade used seven pounds of butter in one recipe! My mother never would dream of making pie crust with butter. She uses lard. And then Mrs. Hoade gave all the pies to Dinna for her family. *Gave* them away."

"Well, that was nice of her," said Baldy.

"Yes, but . . . Oh, my. It's too complicated. You don't understand."

"I understand one thing. That lady's lost a few marbles. Nobody makes ten pies."

"The point is that God is testing me," Dorothy said. "He's showing me how wasteful and sinful people who have lots of money are, and yet . . ." Dorothy couldn't finish. And yet, she knew very well, when she got her working papers in two years she'd probably have to have a summer job in a department store or waiting tables, and Baldy, who was neither sinful nor wasteful, would be back here again, giving riding lessons and cantering all over the countryside as if it belonged to her.

"We'll leave all of this for Dinna in the morning," Mrs. Hoade announced with a sweeping gesture. Dorothy surveyed the scene in the kitchen for a moment. Thank heaven she was never asked to clean up.

"Did you check what the girls were watching?"

"George Gobel, I think. There's nothing bad on anyway," Dorothy said, shuffling the index cards before her, her pen in her teeth. Mrs. Hoade walked over to the counter and poured herself what appeared to be the fourth Scotch of the evening. She had used every pot and pan in the kitchen, as usual. "Do you want me to write this out on the legal pad?" Dorothy asked. "About not putting your nose very close to the risen dough before you punch it down or else you'll sear the inside of your nostrils for hours?"

"Don't you think descriptions like that are useful?"

Mrs. Hoade asked, sitting down across the kitchen table from Dorothy.

"I've never seen things like that in a cookbook before," Dorothy said.

"Of course not," said Mrs. Hoade with a very confident smile. "Of course you haven't. And that's what's wrong with most cookbooks. They are not *real*. They're just a collection of ingredients. I want to get the feel, to convey texture and experience of each of these recipes. I want the reader to be transported to my kitchen. Vita's book, much as I admire it, and you needn't say anything to her tomorrow night, but it's just too organized. It's cold. It hasn't the rough edges of hard, loving work in it. That's why, Dorothy," Mrs. Hoade concluded in a near whisper, "this book is going to be something new!" She smiled at the ice clinking in her glass. "I could have just asked Dinna for the recipes, but I insist on trying them all myself. That's reality. How many cookbooks have you seen, Dorothy, with recipes for more than six or eight people at the very most? The Pennsylvania Dutch have very large families. They cook, every day of the week, for all the men who work in the fields. The women get up at four A.M. to start their baking. This is real life, not some dictator's palace full of Chinese slaves. By the way, I'm changing the title to *Amish Surprise!*"

"Is Dinna Amish?" Dorothy asked.

"No, but it's all right. The word *Amish* is more eye-catching and individual than the word *Pennsylvania*." Mrs. Hoade drained the rest of her drink in a quick gulp.

"We'll let Doubleday decide that. I'm going to bed. It's been a hard day and we have an enormous party tomorrow. Did you call the caterer again?"

"Yes," said Dorothy, fishing around under the cookbook notes for the party notes. "I ordered twenty-four herring in dill sauce. Two dozen avocado cocktails. The melon-prosciutto hors d'oeuvres. Stroganoff for twenty-four. Salad for twenty-four. Pears in wine." She stuck the pen back between her teeth and flipped over the page of the yellow legal pad. "Oh, and they don't make baked Alaska. Only assorted French pastry. I got that. Okay?"

"Perfect," said Mrs. Hoade. "Liquor?"

Dorothy turned to another page. "I have it somewhere. Yes. A case of Bell's Scotch, not the cheap stuff. Twenty bottles of . . . I can't pronounce it . . ."

"Châteauneuf-du-Pape."

"Sha-toe-nuf-doo-pap nineteen forty-nine."

"Right," said Mrs. Hoade.

"And all the rest. It's all coming. Here's your list," said Dorothy. "Mrs. Hoade?"

"Yes?"

"Why would anyone put a pear in wine?"

"You'll see tomorrow," said Mrs. Hoade. "By the way, dear."

"Yes?"

"The pen is leaking down your cheek."

Dorothy wiped her mouth on a dish towel. She could hear Mrs. Hoade pour herself one more nightcap, discreetly, from the living-room liquor tray. Bell's. The expensive stuff. Nowhere in this house had Dorothy ever seen a bottle of Four Roses or Seagram's Seven, the two things her father drank. As she stood at the sink, looking out the kitchen window at the big copper beech tree in the middle of the lawn, its bottom branches illuminated slightly by the light from the fountains on either side, the fountains that went on automatically at sundown, she repeated the words, "We'll let Doubleday decide." We! Of course Mrs. Hoade was just using a figure of speech, but still . . . She was a generous woman. She was paying Dinna for the family recipes. I don't want to be paid, Dorothy realized, but to see my name in print. Wow! She found herself grinning. A real book. *Doubleday!* She threw the inky dish towel into the laundry. If I wiped ink on one of Mom's dish towels at home she'd have my head, Dorothy realized suddenly, and at the same moment she thought she understood something. How easy it is, just without thinking, to start acting as if I had all the money in the world. I wonder if Mrs. Hoade once came from a crummy little town like Newburgh. I wonder if she had to get over a million little habits of saving money but never really got over them without feeling a little guilty every time she gives a party or buys a dress. There was no denying that Mrs. Hoade had seemed a bit jumpy. Was that it? Or guilty, that evening after she'd come in from seeing the baby and before she'd sat down to go over the day's notes with Dorothy. She'd handed Dorothy two hundred-dollar bills to pay the caterer tomorrow. Two hundred-dollar bills. Two weeks' salary for her father. Three weeks' salary for Arthur. Dorothy picked the dish towel back out of the laundry basket. She scrubbed at the ink as best she could and hung the towel up to dry.

The crickets chirped outside in the garden and a fresh east wind blew in the window of Dorothy's bedroom. She settled herself on the big mahogany double bed and shoved three pillows under her back. Thirty pages of *David Copperfield*, she instructed herself, then I'll let myself finish that Perry Mason. She reached over to the night table to wind Mrs. Hoade's watch. The watch was not on the night table. It was not on the bureau. It was not on her wrist.

Dorothy squeezed her eyes shut in panic. She slammed *David Copperfield* down on the bed. The watch was probably worth over a hundred dollars. Maybe two hundred, maybe four hundred! Maureen's graduation watch had cost over seventy-five dollars. Had she lost her whole summer's salary? She knew her mother and father would make her pay for it, she knew it was right and decent and moral to pay for it even if Mrs. Hoade didn't insist. Dorothy began to tremble. The watch was no chrome Sears, Roebuck special. It was gold. "I had it at the stable," she said slowly. I remember looking at it there. Could it be in Baldy's car? Baldy dropped me near the end of the driveway. She had the horse van attached today and didn't want to turn around. That was it. She'd had to slam the door three times to get it closed right. Dorothy dressed. Her shirt stuck to the sweat on her back. Her hands shook as they did the buttons. She ran downstairs, let herself out, and traced her steps all the way down the driveway. There was a nearly full moon, but she'd remembered to take a flashlight anyway.

The willow trees brushed her arm as she ran down to the end of the driveway. The night air was delicious, full of perfume from the gardens, but Dorothy noticed none of it. Where did Baldy drop me exactly? Here. There, over there. She knelt down in a ditch by the side of the road. The watch stared up at her solemnly in the moonlight. "Thank you, God, dear Jesus," said Dorothy. Tears streamed down her face. She held the watch in her hands and said the Lord's Prayer. She vowed she'd ask the Hoades to take her to Mass on Sunday. If she had to walk, she'd walk, even if it took all morning; she'd give up a riding day with Baldy. Slowly, now enjoying the soft, fragrant night, she made her way back to the house. I'll finish *David Copperfield* too, she promised, and *Nicholas Nickelby* as well, before I touch another mystery. "Thank you, God!" she shouted to the stars as loudly as she could.

Dorothy took a shortcut past the cottage. Stupid, she told herself immediately, as prickly wild-raspberry runners caught at her ankles. She tripped and fell flat on her face. "Clod! God dammit!" she said. She'd dropped the watch. And I just took God's name in vain, she added to herself. And now I'll never find it. The moonlight did not penetrate the woods here. She turned on the flashlight. The weak beam illuminated something metallic, then something else metallic. When she'd retrieved the watch and thanked God again, she bent over to look at the something else. It was a brass ring, badly corroded, attached to a wooden door. Dorothy stamped. There was a floor beneath her instead of earth. Now go back to the house, Dorothy, she advised herself. Come back tomorrow if you want to have a look. Come back in the daylight. The little house was dark and peaceful. Miss Borg and the baby were no doubt asleep. If she came back tomorrow, Mrs. Hoade might find out. I'll just have a peek, she said as she raised the door. The vines pulled away unwillingly. She flashed the light down into the hole. There's probably a family of water moccasins down here, she thought. Possibly copperheads, or huge black widow spiders. A fairly secure ladder led down, however, and the light from her flashlight bounced down seven ancient but solid steps, as thick as the wood of a telephone pole.

The bottom of the cellar was dry and sandy, not a place for snakes, Dorothy hoped, for leaning against a wood joist was a pair of dusty riding boots. I know what this is, she told herself. This is where the stable used to be. This is the cellar of the old stable! I bet I could shine those boots up even if they are twenty years old. *They don't belong to you, Dorothy. Go back!* she also told herself. She put one foot on the ladder, holding tight to the trapdoor frame as she went down. The step held firm. Thief! Dorothy whispered.

Cautiously she kicked over one boot, then the other. No dead mice in the toes so far. At the other end of the cellar a second ladder reached up to another trapdoor at a place that must have been directly under the cottage. I'd better be quiet or Miss Borg will hear me. As she reached for the boots again, the beam of the flashlight petered out to a weak flicker. She turned around deliberately, like a robot, she told herself, all the while saying, I'm all right. I can see where I came in. I can see up through the open door.

One step at a time. Seven steps and I'll be at the ladder again. Her foot hit against something. She dropped the flashlight. It thudded softly on the earthen floor. Dorothy reached down to feel for it. Then her hand touched another hand, an arm and then a tiny shoulder. It was the body of a baby covered with a kind of slime.

Chapter

———

Five

Nice Miss Borg. Sweet Miss Borg. Miss Borg had not told Mrs. Hoade. Dorothy shook out the frills in the dress she was to iron and Lisa was to wear. Mrs. Hoade was too worried about the clouds that were gathering in the afternoon sky, threatening her party. She had not even noticed the nettle scratches on Dorothy's hands and elbows.

Dorothy did not remember screaming. She did remember the other trapdoor opening, the one that led up to the cottage. In the bright light that had suddenly flooded the cellar, she had seen both Miss Borg and the two stone cupids from the vanished fishponds at once. They lay side by side at her feet, one holding a jug, the other jugless, the two of them covered with a mossy growth. Body of a baby indeed! How she could have mistaken an old limestone statue for the body of a baby, she didn't know, but Dorothy was determined not to let her imagination run away with her like that again. Dorothy had apologized profusely to Miss Borg, remembered the watch, forgotten the boots, and bowed her way up the ladder and out of the cellar like a mandarin.

Dinna clattered the dishes in the kitchen downstairs. Matthew's lawn mower buzzed in the front garden and the birds outside sang and whistled like steam kettles.

"Push it to the right," said Mrs. Hoade, examining the switch on the iron.

"I did," said Dorothy. "It still isn't working."

Mrs. Hoade looked down at her right hand. She held her forefinger and thumb together as if to grasp an invisible pencil. "I'm sorry, the left," she said. "I never can remember which is which and I'm thirty-five years old."

"Mommy, do we have to wear dresses?" Lisa whined.

"Now, honey. This is something *very* special tonight." Mrs. Hoade squinted out at the sky again.

"You always say whatever Daddy does is very special." Jenny joined Lisa whining. "Just like when he was going to start a company and when he brought that man home from Las Vegas that you said was a . . ."

"Jenny!"

"I want to watch *As the World Turns*," said Jenny with a sigh.

"And I want to watch cartoons after that," said Lisa.

Mrs. Hoade smiled impishly at Dorothy. "Do you promise to be good tonight?" she asked them.

"Yes, Mommy," came the answer from both of them.

"And go to bed when Dorothy tells you?"

"Yes, Mommy."

"And try to stay clean in front of Daddy?"

"Yes, Mommy."

"Well, all right, but after that, after those two programs, it will be time to get ready. Are you sure you don't mind ironing, Dorothy?"

"Not at all," Dorothy said, glad for something to do that salved her very guilty conscience. *Stealing*. There was no other word for it. Going down and bothering Miss Borg was bad enough. Breaking Mrs. Hoade's injunctions about going near the old foundations was worse. But almost stealing a pair of riding boots. I would have asked her—Dorothy tried to sound convincing to herself. I would have just brought them up to the house and then asked Mrs. Hoade if I could borrow them. But of course that wasn't true, and she knew it. . . .

Dorothy tried to remember just how her mother dampened cotton voile, exactly how Maureen laid a puffed sleeve on the point of an ironing board. Mrs. Hoade looked on approvingly as Dorothy turned the dress inside out, as if she were trying to learn something. Dorothy was not fooled, but she did wonder, if she were one day to marry a super, rich Englishman like David Niven, whether she too would simply forget all the humdrum things she'd known before, like how to iron a dress.

"Is . . . this man coming down in the same car with

Mr. Hoade?" Dorothy asked, for she now had guessed that "N" was a man as well as a campaign.

"Yes, indeed. They'll do some business on the way down," Mrs. Hoade answered. "I hope it doesn't rain. I hope there isn't traffic. John's always in a . . . bad mood when things go wrong." She twisted her hands a bit and looked out at the sky again.

"I didn't know Mr. Hoade was in politics," Dorothy ventured.

"Politics and advertising are all the same," said Mrs. Hoade. "Actually John is in public relations. That's what he prefers to call it."

"I was hoping," Dorothy said as meekly as she could, "I mean I know how terribly important you said this man is to Mr. Hoade and to you, but if . . . well, I have to do a history term paper next year. It's a big project in second semester and I was wondering if after the girls are in bed if I could just meet . . . or say I had interviewed a famous political . . ."

"Of course!" interrupted Mrs. Hoade. "Now I'd better see what Dinna is doing. And Matthew ought to have brought in the flowers by now. I'll tell John and I'm sure anybody you'd like to talk to tonight will only be flattered and glad to help you. You have the two hundred I gave you? I'm expecting people to call from the station within the hour and I may be out when the caterer delivers."

"Yes, Mrs. Hoade."

Since that morning, "N" had ceased to be a deodorant or a false-teeth adhesive. "N" was a man running for office, possibly a famous politician. SACRED HEART SOPHOMORE GETS SCOOP ON ELECTION! ran the headline in Dorothy's imagination. Rather than start next term with a black mark against her, she might be able to impress the daylights out of her teachers, terrifying Sister Theresa in particular. Sister Theresa, according to legend, had once kept a boy out of Notre Dame because he'd written on his final exam that Henry the Eighth had married eight wives instead of six. Sister Theresa knew all about Dorothy, of course. All the Sisters would be watching her next year, watching for notes to be passed. If she showed some honest, innocent initiative, the sort of thing Sister Elizabeth always talked about, independent involvement, then perhaps she would be forgiven a little bit.

She was going to listen very carefully tonight. Apparently, if one got hold of politicians at parties, when their guard was down and they'd had a drop too many, one could learn the most amazing things. Dorothy wondered if she should take her exclusive interview to the school paper or the *Journal-American* first. Either way, her teachers would be impressed and her father tickled pink. She decided to wait and see if she could find out anything scandalous. Dorothy Coughlin, Girl Reporter: Dorothy liked the sound of that. It was much more exciting, really, than spending her life writing novels. Much safer and more realistic than being a secret agent. She would have an apartment all her own in New York City or Washington. She would wear one-hundred-dollar suits from Saks Fifth Avenue, and big floppy hats, and carry an alligator bag. She'd have a press card, too. That would guarantee entrance to the Pope himself. Her first assignment, she decided, once she'd been hired by a paper, would be to do an exposé on the senators and their free Scotch.

Dorothy finished the girls' dresses. Eyeing them critically, she hung them on a clothesline in the laundry room. Shoes! she thought. I wonder if their shoes are shined. Mrs. Hoade was as impressed with her thoughtfulness and organization as Dorothy intended her to be. Dorothy was impressed herself. She polished the girls' Mary Janes to a patent-leather glow, laid out their lace-topped socks and clean underwear, and then began on her own clothes. She had only the same cotton dress that she'd worn to every party, but Mrs. Hoade had given her a necklace of amber beads to wear that night and the whole effect was a little dressier.

Poor Mrs. Hoade. When she emerged clumsily from the car, after picking up two people at the train station, she looked so frowsy, so unwell-dressed. Dorothy watched from an upstairs window for a second, before going to bathe the girls. Mrs. Hoade had chosen a dress with enormous white peacocks on a black background. Her hair had not been set. She's probably never had anyone to tell her, Dorothy mused, thinking kindly, for once, of Maureen. Maureen had taught her all about lipstick colors and hairstyles, fat clothes and thin clothes. Mrs. Hoade was hopeless. Perhaps, if I suggest it nicely . . . Dorothy considered, I can help her.

She ran Lisa's bath. In case she got rumpled or splashed,

Dorothy didn't want to dress herself until both girls were totally finished. She'd bribe them with dessert to keep them quiet while she dressed.

"Two éclairs *each*," Jenny made her promise. "Unless they have meringues. If they have meringues and no éclairs we get three meringues with ice cream and chocolate sauce and whipped cream, and if they have both, we get one of each apiece."

Lisa upped the ante to one éclair and three meringues.

"We'll just have to see," said Dorothy, soaping Lisa's knees. "I'll do the best I can."

A door slammed downstairs. She heard Mr. Hoade's voice, then many other voices. Ice tinkling in glasses. Someone laughing.

After a few minutes, Mr. Hoade came bounding up the stairs and walked into the bathroom.

"Daddee!" said Lisa.

"Daddy's little princesses!" he said, squatting down. He straight-armed a dripping Lisa away from him. "No!" he said. "Don't you get Daddy's new tux all wet!" Lisa's face puckered up as if she were going to cry. Mr. Hoade stood up and cracked all the knuckles in his fingers. "How are you doing, honey?" he asked Dorothy.

"Fine, thank you, Mr. Hoade," said Dorothy as she dried Lisa.

"That's good. Here," he said, producing a photograph from his jacket pocket. "My wife tells me you wanted this." He turned and loped away down the stairs as quickly as he'd come.

Dorothy stared at the face. She didn't recognize it. "Best Wishes to Dorothy," the inscription ran. She'd never heard of the name either. Best Wishes indeed!

Politics, national and local, was the most discussed subject at her parents' dinner table. Dorothy's mother wasn't overly interested, but politics for her father was an obsession and love. Although he never said so, Dorothy sensed he'd been disappointed that Kevin had not gone to law school, and Terrance had only a football scholarship. He would have loved it if either of them had run for office. Dorothy knew, without a doubt, that this man with the fleshy, drooping jowls and the slicked back hair had never been in newspapers she'd seen and she'd never heard his name mentioned even once, so he must be pretty small potatoes. Even if he was small potatoes, he might have been interesting, but if he thought Dorothy was just another autograph-seeking teenager, he'd never say anything important to her. He'd probably pat her on the head and ask how she was doing at school. Her heart sank. "Now wait in your room till I'm finished," she told Jenny and Lisa irritably.

"Remember," said Lisa. "Two éclairs apiece. Not one each."

"I said I'd do the best I could," snapped Dorothy.

"You promised!" Lisa whined.

"I did not! And if you keep that up you won't get anything at all!"

See if I care, she grumped as she combed her hair. Still, perhaps things weren't that gloomy. If she could find out how advertising controlled political campaigns, even small ones, it might make a good paper for Sister Theresa. If she could uncover some scandalously misrepresented issues, it might be of interest to some newspaper. After all, she told herself, you have to start somewhere.

She heard a terrible shriek from downstairs. It was Lisa. Dorothy dropped her comb and flew out of her room.

She brushed past Jenny, who stood mutely on the stairway, watching her sister. Lisa's fingernails were dripping nail polish all over the rug, her shoes, and her freshly ironed dress.

"You got it on my *pants*!" Mr. Hoade was saying to her between his clenched teeth. "Dorothy, get down here!" he yelled as Dorothy ran downstairs. "Look what has happened! I thought you were paid to watch the girls!"

Where was Mrs. Hoade? Would she be angry after having been so nice all day? She'd even let Dorothy take the morning off to go riding. Dorothy could see her outside in the garden with the guests. "I'm sorry, Mr. Hoade. I just had to take five minutes and get ready myself. I couldn't come down in dungarees in front of all these . . ."

"You are paid to watch the girls, not to fuss with your own hair!"

"She said three meringues!" Lisa sobbed out. "And then she went back on her word!"

"What's this about meringues?"

Dorothy took a deep breath. "All I said, Mr. Hoade,

was if the girls were good I'd get them some French pastry. I didn't think . . ."

"You bribed them, is that it?"

"Two éclairs and three meringues!" Lisa yelled.

"I said I'd do the best I could, Lisa," Dorothy began.

"Then you said we wouldn't get anything at all!" Lisa's words were nearly unintelligible. Mr. Hoade had marched off into the kitchen in search of kerosene.

"Dorothy's right," came a voice from the stairway. "And you know it, Miss Wet-Bed!"

Dorothy stopped Lisa's lunge just short of Jenny, who'd come sashaying down and was now walking unconcernedly out the door to the garden. "If you get Dorothy into trouble, we won't get anything, stupid!" was Jenny's parting shot.

"I'll get you! I'll get you!" screamed the surprisingly strong little girl.

"Easy . . . easy," said Dorothy as if to a shying horse. Dorothy held her around the middle firmly, but with one tremendous spasm, Lisa bit Dorothy on the wrist and sent them both tumbling backward into the silver liquor tray. Dorothy's shoulder smashed into the side of the portrait that hung above the tray, but mercifully the painting did not shift in the slightest or swing out into the pointed corner of the breakfront as she had feared, or fall into the broken glass of the sherry decanter that lay at her feet.

"Give her to me!" said Mr. Hoade from the kitchen doorway. "Hold her there," he instructed Dorothy. Dorothy, her good cotton dress soaked in sherry, with

Lisa writhing like a tiger in her lap, sat motionless and watched as Mr. Hoade strode over and hovered above them. "You're going to get a licking for that. Oh, yes, you are!" he shrieked, taking off his jacket and rolling up his sleeve.

"John, please!" It was Mrs. Hoade, who'd run in from the garden, breathless.

"I don't give a damn what you say," he growled. "She's going to be punished. Look what she did to my pants! Look what she did to Doris's arm!"

"It's *Dorothy*," said Mrs. Hoade.

"She could sue us!"

"I won't sue anybody! I promise," Dorothy said, sweeping Lisa up in a bundle in her arms. She carried Lisa upstairs. "It'll be all right. I'll just get her cleaned up."

Dorothy glanced down miserably to the runny pink stains and sticky blotches that coursed down her good dress and made the cloth adhere uncomfortably against her legs. Soapy lather did not improve the mess Lisa had made of her fingernails. Lisa's tantrum had ebbed completely, but in its stead was something close to a wordless panic. Holding Lisa like a wounded puppy, Dorothy sat down on the fluffy hamper lid and rocked her in her lap. She sang her a lullaby her mother had made up and used when Dorothy had been little. Lisa's pink thumb went into her mouth and she closed her eyes. Dorothy hoped she could transmit some peace to the little girl as easily as Mr. Hoade had imparted terror.

"Let's try another bath," she said, when Lisa's breathing steadied.

"I had a bath already."

"I know. I know, but it isn't just to get you clean. It's also . . . Well, when I'm upset about something I sit in a hot tub. It makes me feel much better." Dorothy drew the bath water. "And while you're sitting in it, we'll play Twenty Questions. How would that be?"

"I guess so," said Lisa, her voice shaking a little.

"Now get in so you don't catch cold. Does Mommy have any nail-polish remover?"

"I don't know."

"Where did you find the nail polish?"

"In her top bureau drawer."

"Okay. Now while I get it, you think of the nicest thing in the whole world, okay?"

"What is that?" asked Lisa, lowering herself into the bubbles.

"Anything you want it to be," said Dorothy. She closed the bathroom door so that Lisa would not be in a draft, and went off in search of nail-polish remover.

Mrs. Hoade didn't seem to be the type to wear nail polish in the first place. Her nails were bitten and the cuticles overgrown. Dorothy opened the top drawer, inhaling as she did the sweet, nostalgic smell of lavender sachet. Curiously enough there were at least five bottles of nail polish, all the same color, Windsor, lined up against the side of the drawer. Fortunately there was a bottle of remover at the end of the row. Under the bottles, along with combs, powder puffs, a key ring, the gold locket Mrs. Hoade usually wore, an embossed silver pencil, a reading magnifier, and all sizes of emery boards, was a stack of photographs in a yellow envelope. Underneath that was a pile of letters. Dorothy glanced guiltily over her shoulder. She felt curiosity overcome her as surely as the tide taking an unmoored boat out to sea.

The envelope had been processed by Kodak in the fall of 1944. She was about to look furtively at what she hoped were old love letters underneath, when she thought she'd see if there were any pictures of the stable. She flipped through the photographs. Sure enough, the stable stood right about where the cottage had been built. She could tell by the presence of an ash tree that still grew in the very same spot. The stable had been built of board-and-batten siding, Dorothy told herself proudly. Sister Elizabeth's English classes covered a whole range of what Sister considered an educated young man or lady should know. There was a hayloft and a cistern right near the entrance. There were several pictures of horses, but the people seated upon them or holding their lead lines were too small to identify. She came upon a picture of the fishponds as well, and saw the cupids once again. They looked so fine and innocent in the sunlight. Dorothy was sorry that they should now be buried away in the cellar like dead bodies. There were a few interior shots of the house. One showed the greenhouse from the inside. Instead of the present living-room wall, where the painting hung and the highboy stood, there was no wall at all, only a pleasant vista of sunlit glass and aspidistras sitting in wrought-iron planters. Otherwise, nothing but the wall-paper seemed to have changed downstairs.

"Dorothy, come!" Lisa's muffled voice called to her from the bathroom. What a shame that stable was destroyed, Dorothy thought as she stuffed the pictures back in the envelope.

Lisa sat in the bubbles, smiling and composed when Dorothy reached the bathroom. She extended a dreadful pink hand and placed it on the rim of the tub for Dorothy to clean, and grinned as if nothing had happened. "Did you think of the nicest thing in the whole world?" Dorothy asked.

"Yup."

"What was it?"

Lisa looked up slyly and grinned. "Two éclairs," she said, "and three meringues with chocolate sauce and whipped cream and ice cream."

No trace of a stain remained on Mr. Hoade's trousers when Dorothy came out into the garden, her traveling skirt and blouse replacing the cotton dress. With the disappearance of the nail polish his anger, too, seemed to have vanished. Maybe he swallowed some of the kerosene, Dorothy thought. I wish he had.

"This is my little princess!" he said, scooping up a pristine Lisa now outfitted in a slightly outgrown yellow dress and presenting her to the flaccid-jowled gentleman whose signed photograph now adorned the inside of Dorothy's wastebasket. They must have retouched out half his chins in the picture, she decided.

"I'm Dorothy Coughlin, sir," she said boldly. "I'm very honored to meet you." Mr. Hoade did not look pleased.

"Are you the little girl who wanted the autographed picture?" he asked, taking a large black cigar out of his mouth and grinning broadly. He was wearing a vest, Dorothy noticed, and trousers with front pleats, so he was probably a Republican. If there was to be a scandal, all the better.

"Yes, sir. I was hoping, if you had a minute, sir . . . I'm the editor of our high-school newspaper," Dorothy lied headily, "at Sacred Heart in Newburgh, and I'm going to be a reporter someday and I was wondering if I could ask you some questions on the coming campaign . . . I . . . I certainly would appreciate it and I'm sure everybody at school would appreciate it too, that is . . . if it isn't too much trouble."

"Shoot!" said the toothy, cigar-filled mouth. The pale blue eyes called off Mr. Hoade's intervention with an amused blink.

"Well, sir," said Dorothy, her mouth drying up. "May I ask what office you're running for?"

"President."

"President!"

"You heard it right."

Dorothy tried to swallow. If this man was running for president, it was beyond her wildest dreams. She had counted on governor or even senator, but president! "And what," she heard herself ask, "is your position, sir, on . . . on the Russians?" she managed to blurt out.

The cigar was removed again.

"You mean the longshoremen's strike?"

"Longshoremen's strike?"

"Yes, the dockers' boycott."

"Yes . . . that one."

"Well, I support them, naturally, but that's a different union, you know."

"A different union?"

"Honey?"

"Yes, sir?"

"Did you think I was running for president of the United States?"

"Uh . . . no!" said Dorothy.

"John, what have you been telling people?" The mouth and the four fat chins began to jiggle in tremendous merriment. The laughing voice went abruptly serious again, however, and to Dorothy's disappointment informed her that the presidency in question belonged to a labor union, but if Dorothy was interested in finding out about the Russians, she should write a letter to Congressman Such-and-such from the second district in Philadelphia, mention his name, and she would get a personal reply to all her questions. As soon as this advice was given, Mr. Hoade steered Dorothy to the buffet table, placed a dinner plate in her hands, and with a sarcastic bow disappeared into the crowd of people.

There was nothing on God's green earth, Dorothy

thought sadly as she helped herself to some beef Stroganoff, that was more boring or unglamorous than labor unions. Her father belonged to the P.B.A., and she hated it when he talked of the tiresome meetings he attended and the gray-faced, ill-spoken men who ran them.

Lisa and Jenny, uninterested in the Stroganoff, found their way to the television early. "This is all I could get you," said Dorothy, presenting them with two soggy cream puffs. "There were no éclairs and no meringues."

"We saw," said Lisa.

"What are you watching?" Dorothy asked.

"*Return of the Cat People,*" Lisa answered, "and Mom said we could."

Lisa's singsong assertiveness convinced Dorothy that she was back to normal after the tantrum. She left both girls and went into her own room with the intention of losing the earlier humiliations of the evening in Istanbul, or wherever Agatha Christie would take her.

Perhaps, she thought, as she settled herself on the bed, a slowly melting cream puff on the dresser, I'll be able to wangle a ride tomorrow. Agatha Christie did not successfully obliterate the memory of the horrid, fat jowls, or the mocking laughter she'd endured. And all my fault, Dorothy told herself. She wished she'd brought the pair of riding boots back and could have spent the evening cleaning them up. After all, she reasoned, I could tell Mrs. Hoade that Baldy gave them to me. It isn't stealing to take something that nobody wants or even knows is there. "Oh, yes, it is!" said Maureen. "It's stealing and it's lying!" "Suspicion always haunts the guilty mind!" cautioned Sister Elizabeth. "The thief doth fear every bush an officer!" The source of that wisdom escaped Dorothy. Sister had used it every day in class for two weeks until Michael Brodie finally returned a five-dollar bill he claimed he'd found on the ball field, but that everybody knew he'd slipped out of Mary Beth Pendleton's desk when she wasn't looking.

I didn't lose the watch after all, she went on, trying still to concentrate on her book, and Miss Borg was good enough not to rat on me. I'm grateful. God has been merciful, and look what I'm doing. I'm still thinking about stealing those boots. I'm the best example of a miserable sinner I can think of, Dorothy decided. Maureen's absolutely right. I'll probably wind up in jail someday. Mrs. Hoade could fire me for stealing. That would look just dandy at home, wouldn't it. She went back to Istanbul.

Dorothy read three pages. She turned back to the beginning of the story. She'd forgotten what was going on. Baldy's riding breeches (not the same as jodhpurs, as she had been told by Baldy) had an elegant look. They were enhanced, even on chubby Baldy, by the soft leather and potent shape of her old mahogany-topped hunting boots. Dungarees and loafers, despite Dorothy's svelte figure, made her feel silly and amateurish next to Baldy. The boots would help, even without the breeches. The girls would be busy with their *Cat People* for at least another hour. The party would go on down at the swimming pool, far from the cottage, until midnight, surely. As usual, Dorothy remembered to lock her door before she went out, in case Lisa sneaked in to go through her things and discovered she wore a 32A instead of a 34B bra.

Thunder rattled somewhere miles away. A strong wind blew a cloud in front of the moon, extinguishing its light, hiding Dorothy as her feet scudded through the mounds of newly mown grass. She hadn't been able to find any more flashlight batteries, but had managed to locate a candle and a book of matches. I'm not frightened, she told herself. The cloud moved away and then moonlight broke out again, lighting the tops of the grasses around the narrow path to the cottage. Not a bit frightened. After all, if I were an archaeologist I'd have to do a lot of things scarier than this. There had been a time, that past winter after Sister Elizabeth had gone off on a tangent and spent a whole class talking about Heinrich Schliemann and the discovery of Troy, when Dorothy had made a final decision to become an archaeologist. She and Kate had written to the Museum of Natural History to apply for summer jobs on a dig anywhere in the world. The Museum had responded politely that they were much too young, but Dorothy still had it in her mind to discover a lost city in the East someday. Think of Heinrich Schliemann, she told herself as the trees rustled around her. He wouldn't be afraid of snakes and spiders in some silly old basement in Pennsylvania. Once she stopped and peeked through the brush to the faraway party. All she could see were the Japanese paper lanterns swinging wildly in the wind like captive balloons. I can still go back, she said, mentally shaking a finger at herself. Greed is pushing me forward. My good conscience is weak. Dear God, let me get the better of this.

The thunder rattled again, not so distant this time. The little house looked dark and comfortable ahead of her. She rummaged around in the vines and nettles for several minutes until she found the heavy metal ring again. The trapdoor creaked as it gave and then rose under her urging. She stopped. No light was turned on in the cottage. By now there was enough cracking and soughing of branches to hide her movements anyway. Dorothy placed her right foot on the first rung of the ladder. I'll tell Mrs. Hoade, she resolved. I'll tell Mrs. Hoade the truth about losing her watch last night, and finding this door, and being very careful not to get hurt. I'll tell her I found the boots and I'll ask her if I may borrow them for the summer. Dorothy sighed. She smiled. If the riding boots could be shined up and made presentable, they would be worth risking Mrs. Hoade's annoyance at her explorations here. She climbed down without hurrying and lit the candle when she reached the floor. The burst of warm friendly light showed the boots, lying on their sides, exactly as she'd left them. She shook each one just to make doubly sure nothing had nested inside. A white deposit fell off the leather onto her fingers; however, it seemed still to be in tolerable condition underneath. Suddenly a massive clap of thunder echoed outside. The cellar would be a good place to wait out the storm, Dorothy reckoned; on the other hand, I might be here all night and they may come looking for me. She pinched out her candle and, boots under her arm, crossed the sandy floor to the ladder.

The first of the rain pattered down on her face. She closed the door soundlessly and took refuge under the ash tree as another deafening crash roared overhead. What a stupid place to be in a thunderstorm! she said aloud, holding her hands over her ears. THIEVING MOTHER'S HELPER STRUCK BY LIGHTNING! said the *Daily News* headline in her mind. Dorothy prepared to make a dash for the big house, when the lightning seemed to split open the entire sky. It illuminated the woods and cottage and every blade of grass in an eerie sliver of deadly clarity. Then she saw someone standing at the window of the cottage looking out at the storm. The person was too tall to be Miss Borg.

Chapter

Six

"Daddy, will you play with us today? Will you go swimming with us today?" Lisa asked, pushing the cereal up the sides of her bowl to give it the appearance of having been eaten.

"If I have time, Lisa. I have lots to do. I have to wait for a call from Mommy."

As Dorothy poured herself a second cup of coffee, Mr. Hoade turned to her and remarked, "You're an ambitious type of kid, aren't you?"

"Excuse me, Mr. Hoade?"

"Daddy, when is Mommy coming home?" Lisa asked.

"I told you before, I don't know. Sit down," he said

to Dorothy, "but first get me another cup. Pour the rest of that out. It's cold."

Dorothy set the coffee before Mr. Hoade. She sat. Her head pounded from a nearly sleepless night.

"You really the editor of your school paper?" Mr. Hoade asked.

"Why, yes," Dorothy answered. Lying, she figured, would be easier than explaining why she'd lied.

"Well, you must be the best student in the whole school, then."

"No." She hesitated. "Not really. Why?"

"Because," said Mr. Hoade leaning across the table and smiling slyly, "editors of high-school papers are always seniors!"

"Not at Sacred . . ."

"You interested in politics?"

"Yes, well, I . . ."

"Not in labor unions."

Dorothy took a scalding swallow of coffee. "Well, my Dad belongs to the Policemen's Benevolent Association and it's awfully dull," she said, relieved to be allowed to finish a sentence.

"Daddy, what's wrong with the baby? Why is it sick?" Lisa asked.

"I told you, it's just very sick, that's all. We won't know anything more until Mommy or the doctor calls. Now shut your mouth and eat your breakfast."

"How can I eat my breakfast with my mouth shut?" Lisa whined.

"Do you want Daddy to swim with you?"

Lisa toyed with her spoon. She didn't answer. Mr. Hoade turned back to Dorothy. "I just thought I'd tell you something," he said smugly, leaning back in his chair and folding his hands over his stomach. "If you want to be a reporter, you ought to know one thing."

"What's that, Mr. Hoade?" asked Dorothy, knowing she was supposed to say that and wishing his chair would topple beneath him.

"Power," he continued, lighting a cigarette, "real power, is never where you think it is. It's never where people want you to believe it is. You probably think all these glamor boys who run for office are the people who make things work. Not in a pig's eye," he said, blowing a stream of smoke straight up in the air. "Except for a few committee chairmen in Washington, and the son of a bitch in the White House, union president, this union in particular, is one of the most powerful jobs in the country. But my man doesn't get his picture in the papers unless there's a strike, and he doesn't have his hair done by some monkey from Paris. Someday," Mr. Hoade added after making a face at the dregs in his coffee cup, "you'll know things like that."

"Thank you for telling me," said Dorothy as earnestly as she could.

"You never heard of my man before, did you?"

"No, Mr. Hoade."

"You probably thought you were going to meet somebody like Sparkman or Kefauver, didn't you?"

"Well, I knew his name began with an N, so . . ."

"My man is a whole lot bigger than Sparkman or Kefauver or Stevenson or all of them rolled into one."

"Yes, Mr. Hoade." said Dorothy. She wondered what a "monkey from Paris" was.

"Well, you didn't get very far last night, so you can ask me what you want for your paper."

"Well," she said, swallowing the last of an English muffin, "the only thing I can think of to ask is . . . wasn't that the union that had the trouble recently?"

"What trouble?" he asked coldly.

Dorothy gulped down some more coffee. "Well, um, there was a murder, wasn't there? Of a man who was going to be the president of the union? And there were some witnesses to it? The children's governess, wasn't it? And one of them was killed before the trial? And the other one hasn't ever been found?"

"You know something, honey?" said Mr. Hoade.

"Yes, Mr. Hoade?"

"One of the first things about being a good reporter is getting your facts straight."

"I didn't mean . . . I just thought . . ."

"And if you were a real reporter, instead of a fifteen-year-old kid, and what you just described didn't happen to be in a different union, which it is, and didn't happen to be mixed up with the Lindbergh kidnaping, and you brought up anything like that to me or anybody at the party last night, you know where you'd be right now?"

"No, sir."

"Out of a job with your head in a toilet!"

"Daddy, that's not nice!" said Jenny.

"Excuse *me*!" he said. "You're absolutely right, honey, and don't tell Mommy I said that. But it's true. There's a whole lot of things in this world that aren't so nice, and you know what I'd do if I were you?" he asked Dorothy.

"No, sir."

"I'd go to a nice college and meet a nice boy and have some nice babies and forget about anything else."

"But," Dorothy gasped, "I don't *want* to! I want to *be* somebody!"

Mr. Hoade held his head cocked to one side. A habit of Lisa's, Dorothy noticed. He looked at her keenly and grinned devilishly. "I knew you'd say that," he said.

Sensing an opening, Dorothy plunged right in. "Mr. Hoade, may I ask you something? I mean it's none of my business, I suppose, but I was just curious. You don't have to answer if you don't want, but something is bothering me."

"Like the man said, shoot!"

"Well, do you think it's right to keep a mongoloid baby separated from its brothers and sisters? I mean its sisters? I mean to say, or to ask, is it just a plain old mongoloid, because sooner or later Jenny and Lisa will . . ."

Mr. Hoade drummed his fingers on the table. He looked quickly at both his daughters. "Go up and get your suits on," he told them. "I'll meet you at the pool."

Jenny shrugged and left the table, twisting her hair around her finger. Lisa slid her uneaten cereal into the sink and followed Jenny out. When they had gone, Mr. Hoade turned back to Dorothy. "What exactly did Maria say to you?" he asked.

"You mean . . . Mrs. Hoade?"

"Mrs. Hoade," he repeated slowly, lighting another cigarette.

"She . . . she told me the truth, I guess. That your . . . daughter is a mongoloid. She didn't say that to the girls."

Mr. Hoade leaned across the kitchen table. He tapped Dorothy's gold cross with his fingernails. She jumped. "Curiosity killed the Catholic!" he said and chuckled at his pun.

Dorothy wished her head were clearer. She sat in the empty kitchen, staring at the dirty breakfast dishes. I ought to make myself do them, instead of leaving them for Dinna. Her hand lay shadowless on the cool marble table. Dorothy's head bent, suddenly, like a flower bowed with rain. She slept.

"Where'd you get those boots?" Lisa asked.

"Baldy gave them to me."

"They sure are awful-looking."

"They won't be, when I finish cleaning them up," said Dorothy, scraping at the heel of one boot with a piece of twig. "Why don't you take a swim, Lisa?"

"When did Baldy give them to you?" Jenny asked.

"Yesterday."

"There goes Daddy," said Lisa.

Dorothy turned to see Mr. Hoade driving away. He

was going to the hospital, he'd said with a funny look at Dorothy's riding boots. "Horses, huh?" he'd added.

"How come you didn't have them when you came in from riding last night?" Lisa's voice began to assume a teasing rhythm. Dorothy reddened and clenched her teeth. "I'm gonna tell Mom," said Lisa matter-of-factly.

"Just what are you going to tell your mother?" Dorothy snapped, rubbing the heel of her boot vigorously.

"That you stole them."

"I didn't steal them."

"How come you went out of your room last night? I heard you. And how come you came back into your room after a while with those boots? I peeked out and saw you." Dorothy said nothing. "Are you going to hit me?" Lisa asked. Gladly, Dorothy would have thrown Lisa into the pool and drowned her at that very moment.

"When Baldy drove me home yesterday," Dorothy said, "she dropped me at the end of the driveway because she couldn't turn around with the horse van. We got . . . talking and I forgot the boots. I went out to get them, so there."

"I just thought," said Lisa, "that maybe you'd been poking around where you're not supposed to go. I know there's an old stable cellar around here. It's full of poisonous snakes and black widow spiders. Mom said you could sue us for a million dollars if you got hurt."

"Lisa," Jenny interrupted, "if Mom fires Dorothy, you know who we get?"

"Mom," said Lisa, "that's who."

"Dinna," said Jenny.

Bless you, Jenny, said Dorothy silently. You get an extra cupcake for that. She polished carefully and lovingly while the two girls played Go Fish and then Gin Rummy. She wondered if Lisa would, after all, tell her mother about the boots. Well, it didn't matter. Dorothy intended to tell Mrs. Hoade herself when the right moment came. An awful thought crossed her mind. Mr. Hoade had looked curiously at them that morning. Could they have been his boots when he was a boy? There was no difference that she knew between men's and women's riding boots. She would have preferred them to have been worn by a long-dead groom and not have belonged to Mr. Hoade.

"Dorothy?"

"Yes, Jenny."

"Lisa's cheating."

"I am not," said Lisa stoutly.

Play with them, Dorothy, a silent voice instructed. It was Baldy's voice.

"Okay. I'll play with you," said Dorothy, dropping the boot and the polishing rag.

A breeze sprung up, carrying with it the scent of rain and roses. It scattered the playing cards all over the tiles. Several of them blew into the pool. Dorothy jumped in to retrieve them. She swam after the queen of hearts, which had floated down to the deep end. The card turned over in the water and began to sink as her hand reached out for it. She plunged beneath the surface and made another grab for it, but it eluded her and drifted down to the bottom of the pool. Dorothy pulled herself out of the water. She would have to dive for it. For an instant she peered at the queen's passive face through the clear water. Queens on playing cards were dressed something like nuns. As she forced herself down to the deepest part of the pool, right over the drain where the card lay, she realized she was trying to put bits of a puzzle together in her mind.

It had started that morning in the kitchen, when she'd fallen asleep. No, not really, Dorothy corrected herself. It started last night. I thought it was the storm that kept me awake. I wanted it to be the storm. Dorothy rose to the surface of the pool, gasping for breath, queen of hearts in hand. She began plucking the other cards off the water. They had not sunk.

In a queer, unborn dream that had come to her as she had sat slumped over the kitchen table that morning, something had been revealed to her, perhaps some signal. She tried to remember what it was. She'd been sure that she was back in school, sitting in the front row of religion class. Reverend Mother was drilling the class in catechism. Dorothy, in the dream, kept trying not to nod off, but her eyes were too heavy to open and her arms felt paralyzed. She willed them to move, to no avail. In vain she tried to answer Reverend Mother's questions. What were the questions? Dorothy emerged from the pool, cards in a wet stack, and spread them on a towel to dry. Jenny and Lisa watched. What were the questions? Is God all-wise, all-holy, all-merciful, and all-just? No. There was another question. It lay, like a palpable, visible thing in the very back of Reverend Mother's throat. The dream had become a nightmare because Dorothy had been afraid Reverend Mother's mouth would open, revealing that question, and that the mouth would look like the inside of Jonah's whale, a frightening illustration in an old book of Bible stories. A cavernous mouth, blood red, with a person at the back of the throat.

Now that she was awake, she told herself she was no longer frightened. She groped for what she'd known in the dream but couldn't see now. The gentle wind was stirring an unsaid thing to life on the very bottom layer of her memory.

She began to shuffle the deck. Mr. Hoade's face, drawn and unshaven, swam malevolently before her. If her father had heard him use the vulgar language of that exchange at the breakfast table, he would have punched Mr. Hoade right in the nose and taken Dorothy home. She missed her father, suddenly. She missed his bushy eyebrows and his "Irish temper," as her mother called it, that spent itself quickly and settled all things on the side of the angels.

She dealt out ten cards apiece. "I'm going to get them all wet," Jenny announced. She threw the deck in a puddle on her right-hand side.

"What did you do that for?" Lisa whined.

"Because I know what cards are wet and I can tell them from the back," said Jenny. She placed all fifty-two on the towel. Lisa moaned. Dorothy waited and yawned, her thoughts elsewhere.

Mr. Hoade had certainly been upset at the suggestion of trouble in his precious candidate's precious union. Was it, after all, the union that had been in the papers with the murder? He hadn't seemed too pleased at the reminder that his daughter was a mongoloid, either. Leave well enough alone, Maureen warned her silently. Trouble trouble and trouble will trouble you.

Once again God had smiled upon her. Dorothy mouthed a prayer of thanks as Jenny methodically blotted the cards. Mr. and Mrs. Hoade had not noticed her last night when she'd come in, drenched by the cloudburst. Only Lisa had noticed the boots that she'd hidden in the garden until she was sure the coast was clear. But Lisa's guess about stealing could be easily gotten around. Mrs. Hoade had been too busy with her suddenly washed-out party to bother about Dorothy. Mr. Hoade had been obliged to drive his quadruple-chinned client all the way to Philadelphia in the storm. The rest of the guests, in a procession of a dozen cars, had left shortly after. So much confusion. Mr. Hoade had probably not returned until early that morning. He was no doubt exhausted and in a bad mood. Dorothy knew she had an overactive imagination. Even Sister Elizabeth, who was very fond of imaginations, had told her that.

Jenny dealt the wet cards and announced, "Go fish." Dorothy picked up her hand and yawned again.

She would just shut down that busybody in the back of her mind. The Hoade baby probably had meningitis, or something else that tactful Mrs. Hoade didn't want to go into. It might be horribly birthmarked, with dreadful purple streaks all over it. Perhaps it had caught leprosy in the womb in South America and its fingers and toes were dropping off. Lisa and Jenny, if they saw it, would be traumatized for the rest of their lives.

"Do you have any . . . tens?" Lisa asked Dorothy.

"No," said Dorothy. The wind blew a dead rose blossom across the deck of cards. The memory of the dream began to open again, like a fan.

"You do so have tens. You have two tens!" said Lisa irritably, peering over the top of Dorothy's hand, and the image folded in on itself again, leaving Dorothy only with the certainty that whatever it was lay in Mrs. Hoade's top bureau drawer.

Ever since Mrs. Hoade had informed her, without going into detail, that the baby had died in the hospital early that morning, Dorothy had been carrying on a private war with herself. On the one hand she couldn't get the drawer, the thing in the drawer, whatever it was, out of her mind. On the other hand, Maureen's voice, Reverend Mother's voice, a hundred voices including her own good conscience, warned her that she had already transgressed and must go no further. "O what a tangled web we weave, when first we practise to deceive!" cautioned Sir Walter Scott in Sister Elizabeth's flawless impression of a Midlothian burr.

The girls sat in the library, with Dorothy between them, mesmerized by *Lassie*. Mr. and Mrs. Hoade were downstairs in the living room. Mrs. Hoade's face had been ashen since she'd come in. Dorothy prayed her own voice had conveyed enough reverence for the dead when she'd asked if there was anything she could do to help. She could keep the girls entertained. Well, that was what she'd been hired to do. The hamburger tasted dry and uninteresting. Dorothy bit her lip. She'd eaten meat last night. Last night had been Friday.

Suddenly Dorothy longed for the quiet darkness of the confessional. She wanted to wipe out all the nasty suspicions that had gone through her mind that morning. There's just hardly any good in me, she thought. I wish I were like my mother. I wish I were kind and gentle.

"What are you sighing for?" Jenny asked.

"Oh, I was thinking of your parents. I wish I could help them and make them feel better," said Dorothy. Jenny turned back to the television without saying anything. Ice clinked in the silver ice bucket in the living room.

Dorothy knew she could do nothing for Mrs. Hoade. She wondered if she could do anything for herself. Could she obliterate the things she'd seen in herself these past weeks that she really didn't like very much? All her greedy ambitions for illustrious careers? Careers without the hard work; silly, romantic ambitions for fame and fortune at someone else's expense. She wished she could erase all her impatience with poor Jenny and Lisa, whose parents paid them so little attention. She wished she could destroy her envy, covetousness, as Reverend Mother called it, of the Hoades and everything they owned. What had all their money bought them when the chips were down? Nothing. Their baby had died, just like any poor baby in India—or in Ireland, a century before, during the potato famine there.

The closest that she, Dorothy, had ever been to any sort of tragedy was right now, fifty feet away downstairs. She could hear the Hoades moving about, she could hear the ice in their drinks, tinkling almost gaily. She remembered the power of Mrs. Hoade's grief, the tremble in Mrs. Hoade's hands, and Mr. Hoade's red, sleepy eyes.

A little bleakly, Dorothy came to the conclusion that she would never become a reporter, or a spy, or a famous writer. She would do well, when she got home, to be less critical of Maureen, to be more helpful and loving with Bridget. Supposing one day she were to have a baby of her own and that baby were to die. And supposing she'd hired some teenager who poked her nose into everything, looked in drawers, considered reading private letters, and arrived at preposterous conclusions on the basis of spite, envy, and laziness. Who threw away an autographed picture in the wastebasket, for anyone to come upon, just because it wasn't of a person famous enough to suit her snooty tastes. She'd gone three times where she'd been told not to go. What did she know about lawsuits? Perhaps her father *would* sue the Hoades if anything happened to her. Not only had she disobeyed Mrs. Hoade, kind Mrs. Hoade who might put her name in a book, but she'd stolen a pair of riding boots. Well, she was just not going to wear those boots, even if they did look terrific. She was going to ask Mrs. Hoade not to put her name down or acknowledge any help on the cookbook in print.

All the Hoades had shown her, after all, was kindness. She had met wonderful, sparkling people at their parties. She'd ordered hundreds of dollars worth of fancy food for them, and eaten half of it. She'd learned to ride and had been given generous time to do so. The Hoades didn't expect her to do a lick of housework. She didn't even have to make her bed—Dinna would do it. And how had Dorothy repaid the Hoades? Shabbily, she told herself. With a multitude of sins and ugly thoughts. By wishing Mr. Hoade dead on at least two occasions. By insulting his associates, by wishing Lisa dead at least four times that summer, once that very morning when the Hoades' baby was off in a hospital, dying. Dying, for all she knew, in great suffering. Reverend Mother's voice, at its most provoked, flooded her conscience. "Submit yourselves therefore to God. Resist the devil and he will flee from you!"

She decided to give herself a penance of ten Hail Marys and one Our Father for every sin she'd committed and no cheating on the sins by lumping them together. Using the buttons of her shirt for a rosary, she kept up her prayers, right through the whole of *Playhouse 90*. By the time she tucked the girls into bed, Dorothy had finished eighty Hail Marys and eight Our Fathers. As she said good night and closed their door, she remembered about eating meat on Friday and missing Mass and Confession for so many weeks. She said twenty more.

The Hoades were talking quietly in the living room. Dorothy decided not to disturb them. Determined to tackle *Ivanhoe*, she strode with a tranquil heart at last down the hall to her room. She felt so strong now, so happy, so determined to spend the rest of this summer being modest instead of proud, passive instead of prying, that she put her hand to her heart. There she felt what she guessed might be the beginnings of forgiveness and something close to universal love. "The Lord ruleth me," she murmured as she passed the door of the Hoades' bedroom: "and I shall want nothing." She paused for a moment and listened to the rhythm of the conversation downstairs. Dorothy, DON'T! she told herself, almost aloud. But it was too late. She had already gone into their room, opened the drawer, and begun to search for whatever it was that had eluded her thoughts that morning.

Nothing had been disturbed. The odor of sachet, the same Windsor nail polish, the same dark-yellow photo envelope . . . The gold locket was still there. Dorothy picked it up and opened it. A tiny picture of a man's face popped out and fell back into the drawer. She recognized Mrs. Hoade's father from the photo downstairs. On the back of the photograph was written in purple ink, "Krasilovsky 12–6–48." Dorothy smiled. She counted back eight years—1948. So Maria Hoade had once been Maria Krasilovsky. Well, that was something. Dorothy wondered if the now-transformed Miss Krasilovsky had once come from a place as dull and poor as Newburgh, New York. She licked the dry glue and replaced the picture exactly as it had been before, then snapped the locket closed. The name and date and the serious face were not what she was looking for.

Dorothy rummaged through the rest of the drawer's contents. There was a jade-handled letter slitter that looked quite lethal, the emery boards, two pencils—both embossed silver and both leadless—a reading magnifier with a light that didn't work, assorted Indian-head pennies, and a few stamps. There wasn't a single thing that Dorothy could see that fused itself to that slippery idea that had made her look in this drawer again. The only thing left was the stack of letters. She closed the drawer and listened in the hallway again. The Hoades were deep in liquor and conversation; besides, if they did decide to come up, she'd have plenty of warning as the stairs creaked so horribly.

She stepped back to the bureau and thought about the letters. Poking through nail files and old junk was one thing. Looking at people's private mail was another. Still . . . She opened the frayed ribbon that kept the papers in a neat stack. The first was a bill, dated several years before, from the We-Get-Em Exterminating Company. It simply listed "insects—kitchen" and "rodents—cellar" and came to a sum of thirty-eight dollars. The rest were all old bills too. One from a dairy, several from a grocery, and several from a local dry cleaners'. All the papers were equally uninteresting to Dorothy. Newspaper clippings, lists of plant foods for specific kinds of plants, lists of Christmas presents to names that Dorothy didn't know. The last paper in the stack was on memo paper that had printed on it "Don't forget!" The message was *Rotate all four tires on the station wagon.* Not a love letter among them. Not a personal item of any kind. Not anything she was looking for at all.

She stared at her own face in the mirror for a moment. *Something is wrong here, in this place, in this house,* she told herself. *Something is very wrong, I can feel it tingling all around me in the air.* There was a creak on the stairway. Dorothy put out the light and rushed for the doorway, realizing as she did that the hall light was still on and she would be seen coming out the bedroom door. She went the other way, into the Hoades' bathroom, and vanished into Jenny's cave. The fretwork door shut beside her, Dorothy crouched and prayed.

Dear God, please forgive me. I know You are punishing me for looking in that drawer. For breaking my word to You. It was a mortal sin and I know it. Oh dear Jesus, You can strike me dead on the spot if I ever do such a thing again, I promise, but please, please don't let them open this closet door. Our Father who art in heaven. Hallowed be Thy name. . . . She heard Mr. Hoade drop himself into a leather chair not two feet away. They were separated only by the bathroom wall. "What's that, what are you putting away?" she heard Mrs. Hoade ask him.

"Death certificate, autopsy report, doctor's bill, emergency-room bill, pathologist's bill," Mr. Hoade answered.

"How much?" she asked.

"All together? Five eighty."

Mr. Hoade dropped his shoes into the closet with a bang. Some paper was torn in the room. "What's that look on your face?" Dorothy heard him ask.

"Meticulous people have copies of everything," Mrs. Hoade answered.

"Listen, I've checked and I'm telling you no such thing exists!" he said in a barely controlled whisper. "I've checked and we're home free. All right?"

"All right," said Mrs. Hoade at last, in a low, reluctant tone.

He went on in a faintly discernible staccato. "Borg, if you're worried, is hardly in a position to bring anything out now." This was followed by a short laugh. There was no more discussion. Someone came into the bathroom.

The light cord was pulled in the middle of Dorothy's fourth recitation of the Apostles' Creed. Tiny octagons of light filtered through the wicker latticework. Jenny had a lovely hideout here. Several books dug into Dorothy's back and the piggy bank pushed up against her ankle in the corner. "Maker of heaven and earth," said Dorothy, pressing herself as far back against the wall as she could.

She could see nothing. She could not tell whether it was Mr. or Mrs. Hoade who stood at the sink brushing their teeth, or who it was using the john. As the water flushed with an unseemly racket Dorothy gritted her teeth. She would have given all four hundred dollars of her salary to be able to go to the bathroom at that moment. She knew it would be a long while before she dared come out. "The holy Catholic church, the communion of saints, the forgiveness of sins, the resurrection of the body, and life everlasting. Amen," she repeated, digging her fingernails into her palms. She jiggled one leg and then the other imperceptibly. It did not help. Whoever it was left the bathroom and another pair of bare feet padded in.

The water in the sink ran unbearably again. This is my test, Dorothy told herself, please God, let it be my only punishment. Her bladder ached with repression, her shoulder throbbed where she'd hit it the night before, and her back agonized against the pointed corners of Jenny's books.

"Give us this day our daily bread." A toothbrush was banged against the sink. "And forgive us our trespasses." The light was switched off and the plumbing flushed almost all in one motion, although the person had not used the john. "As we forgive those who trespass against us . . . forever and ever." The house turned silent once more. She hadn't actually heard the person leave the bathroom. Could someone be out there, knowing she was in the closet, waiting for her to come out? Dorothy started on her catechism.

She could discern a faint rising and falling of breath, a tiny snore in the next room. After a length of time that defeated Dorothy's whole sense of time, she thought she ought to open the door. Surely no one could stand in the bathroom that long and not make a noise. Bit by bit she pushed the door open. The night was cloudy, but after the pitch-dark blackness of the closet she could see enough, in whatever little light the small bathroom window afforded, to know that no one was there.

She tried not to think of that little devilment that had bubbled up and around her catechism the whole time she had sat waiting. I just want to get to my own bathroom and my own room, she told herself. But why had the john been flushed if it had not been used? "Kleenex. Just a piece of Kleenex," she whispered back at her own questions. Fleetingly her hand explored the floor beside the john. Nothing. But wait. There was something. A piece of paper, two, just under the lid.

"You're safe now, Dorothy," she said with a sigh when she sat on the soft linen sheets of her own bed. Grasped in one hand were two small bits of paper. "Stop, now, Dorothy," she said in a low whisper. "This is their business, not yours, and even if there were something fishy going on, which there almost certainly isn't, just suppose there were, and you found out about it. Do you know where you'd wind up?" Mr. Hoade's voice answered for her. "Out of a job with your head . . ." She squeezed her eyes shut and walked over to her window in a very businesslike manner.

The first bit of paper was blank on both sides. She tore it into infinitesimal pieces anyway. Dorothy the busybody, she hoped with all her might, had disappeared forever. Dorothy the sane, mature young adult had emerged at last. But the second scrap had a word typed on it. The word was *Witnes*—the second *s* torn off, it appeared.

Nothing stirred in the house or on the cool rain-soaked grounds. Not even the moon, when it broke through the clouds and suffused Dorothy's bed with extraordinary light, brought her to the surface of sleep. A barn owl hooted softly, somewhere in the woods. Down in the garden, beneath Dorothy's window, the tiny shreds of both papers rested among the petals of a delphinium.

Chapter

Seven

"Dorothy?"

"Yes, Maureen? How are you?" Dorothy gripped the receiver tightly. She knew just how Maureen was and just what Maureen was going to ask. She hadn't talked to Maureen in two weeks, not since the day after she'd spent the awful few hours in the Hoades' bathroom closet, not since the day of the baby's burial. She'd called Maureen then because she'd been frightened. Now Maureen was going to call in her chips, Dorothy just knew it.

"Have you asked if you can get Labor Day off?"

"Well, no, but I will."

"Dorothy?"

"Yes, Maureen?"

"Two weeks ago to this day you called me up," said Maureen in a voice as measured as a drumbeat. "You wanted my help. You told me all that silly stuff about hiding in a closet and asked me a bunch of fiddle-faddle about labor unions. The minute you get into trouble you come to your sister, right? Isn't that right?"

"Yes, but . . ."

"No buts. It was an act of Christian charity, if you ask me, for me to advise you to stay on your job. I could have very well played on your silly, baseless fears, couldn't I? I would have much preferred you to come home and give me a hand here, but instead I told you to stick to your commitment and stay on the job, didn't I? To my own disadvantage, didn't I?"

"Yes, Maureen."

Mrs. Hoade stepped out of the kitchen. "Almost ready to begin, Dorothy," she said. "Whenever you're ready."

"Right," said Dorothy to Mrs. Hoade. "All right, Maureen. I'll come on Labor Day," she replied into the receiver.

"Well, that's more like it," said Maureen. Dorothy could have kicked herself for making that silly phone call while the Hoades had gone off to the baby's burial. She had waited at the window until Matthew had started up the station wagon. Mr. and Mrs. Hoade had climbed in the front seat with him. It had been pouring rain. She had watched the sheets of water wash over the top of the old brown wood-sided Plymouth, over the end of the shiny black metal coffin that extended out onto the open tailgate. There had been a metal angel stuck to the back of the coffin sobbing over its lyre, wings spread like the wings of an eagle on a silver dollar. Dorothy grimaced at the memory of that awful angel. "Bridget's fine," Maureen was saying.

"Maureen, I have to go. Mrs. Hoade is calling me," Dorothy interrupted.

"We have two and a half minutes left," said Maureen pleasantly. "I got a letter from Mother and one from Kevin." Dorothy hoped Mrs. Hoade wouldn't mind her going home a day early. Everything had been so fine lately. I guess I do owe a debt of thanks to my sister, really, Dorothy told herself. Maureen had scoffed at Dorothy's fears. She'd point-blank refused to go to the newspaper or the library and find out which labor union had been involved in a year-old scandal. She'd told Dorothy to mind her own beeswax, to come home with four hundred dollars or Daddy'd have her head, and to take advantage of night rates if she called collect again. Score one for Maureen, Dorothy thought as she listened to the latest injustice to which Arthur had been subjected. If it hadn't been for my silly imagination, Dorothy told herself, Maureen wouldn't have had one up on me, and I wouldn't have gotten trapped into Labor Day.

"Are you still riding on those horses?" Maureen wanted to know.

"Yes," said Dorothy, "and it's so terrific! I had the loveliest ride today. I've got a pair of boots and . . ."

"How much did *they* cost?"

"Nothing. I found them."

"You probably took them."

"I *asked*, Maureen," Dorothy lied.

"Well, don't come home with a fused spine."

"Maureen." Dorothy felt herself choke. She tried to bite back the tears that filled her eyes and made her whole mouth ache. She might as well have tried to stop the rain.

"Try to write Mom a little more, too. I've written her twenty-one times and she's only had four letters from you. Time's up. Take care of yourself. Good-bye," said Maureen.

Dorothy looked at the receiver. She listened into the empty line. "Good-bye," she said softly.

"Dorothy?" Mrs. Hoade asked, equally softly, from the kitchen doorway. "Would you like a little drink?"

"No, thank you, Mrs. Hoade," she said, "I'll be fine." Dorothy thought she might like one after all, but liquor affected her thinking badly. She had promised to help Mrs. Hoade with what was to be the *pièce de résistance* of the cookbook, and she didn't want to ruin anything by being light-headed. "Jenny and Lisa!" Dorothy called up the stairs. "Very soon now!"

"We hear you," one of them called back down. Dorothy wiped her eyes, went into the kitchen, put on a clean apron, and sat down at her desk with a stack of blank note cards. She was to observe Mrs. Hoade's actions and record them.

"I wish Dinna was here," said Mrs. Hoade.

"Wouldn't she stay?" asked Dorothy.

"She refused to do anything as complicated as this. At least she made the broth," said Mrs. Hoade hopefully.

"Oh," said Dorothy. According to the French cookbook from which Mrs. Hoade was cribbing, Cold Turkey Gallantine in Aspic took two days all together to make. "Cold Boned Turkey in Amish Jelly" wrote Dorothy at the top of the first card. "Is that right?" she asked Mrs. Hoade.

"That's right," Mrs. Hoade answered. "Now watch me carefully." Dorothy watched, pen in hand. Mrs. Hoade made a deep slit with a knife through the length of the turkey.

"Wait!" said Dorothy. Quickly she consulted the cookbook that lay open beside her. "I think you ought to turn it over," she said.

"Why?" asked Mrs. Hoade.

"Well, it says here you're supposed to cut it through the backbone, not the stomach."

"Oh," said Mrs. Hoade. She flopped the twenty-five pound fowl over on its other side. "I hope it doesn't leak," she said. "If it does, I have two reserve turkeys in the icebox. Just in case I make an irreversible mistake."

"We have all evening," said Dorothy. "Let's go slowly. Now, it says remove all the bones without disturbing the skin."

Mrs. Hoade put the turkey down and walked around to stand behind Dorothy and read the cookbook's instructions. Dorothy sat, her eyes on Mrs. Hoade's face, her pen poised. Mrs. Hoade read through two pages of turkey anatomy. "We'll need a pair of pliers to pull the sinews out," she said. "Jenny!"

After a moment, "Yes, Mom?" floated downstairs.

"Get me a pair of pliers, will you please? In the drawer in the hall table." Slow steps thumped down the hall and then down the back stairs.

"I'm going to do it another way," said Mrs. Hoade, sighing at the cookbook. "That way will take all night." Dorothy wrote down *Step One*.

Mrs. Hoade busied herself with the knife for at least ten minutes without speaking. Dorothy wrote down, *Remove all meat from carcass. Discard bones. Place all the pieces of meat according to the bone they came off of* (sic, *better grammar*) *in neat stacks on another table.*

Jenny came in with the pliers. She plopped them down on the table with a loud clank. "Did you save me any apples?" she asked.

"In the icebox," said Mrs. Hoade. "Next to the cream." Jenny took two green apples and walked back upstairs to the library.

"Now," said Mrs. Hoade. She brushed her hands clean on her apron. "I wonder which the sinews are. Well, we'll leave them in for now." She took a needle and thread out of a drawer. "Now, I'm going to sew it back together again," she said.

"You are?" Dorothy asked.

"Much easier," said Mrs. Hoade. She sat in a chair and placed the three bits of meat from the left-hand drumstick together and stitched them into a drumsticklike form. Dorothy wrote *Step Two: Stitch all parts together to retain original shape of the turkey*. "Won't there be a lot of thread when it's finished?" Dorothy asked.

"We'll take it out," said Mrs. Hoade. "Dinna used thread on a chicken cavity last week."

"But don't you think it'll fall apart?"

"The aspic will hold it together," said Mrs. Hoade with a smile.

"But how will we get the thread out through the aspic?" asked Dorothy.

Mrs. Hoade snapped a piece of thread off between her teeth. "I think it will dissolve in the cooking," she answered. Dorothy and Mrs. Hoade sewed the rest of the turkey up as best they could.

"I think I put some breast pieces on the wings," Dorothy admitted.

"Well, it looks nice," said Mrs. Hoade. "Look at that! It looks like a turkey again!"

"It's amazing," Dorothy agreed. She thought she would put a discreet change in her notes. *Use all light-colored thread*, she wrote.

"Jenny! Lisa! Come down now!" Mrs. Hoade yelled, in the meantime squeezing a large wet dish towel.

The girls sauntered into the kitchen after a minute or two. "What's that?" Lisa asked.

"A turkey," said Mrs. Hoade. "Now, Jenny hold one end of the towel and Lisa the other. That's right. Now, here goes the turkey in the middle."

"How can it be a turkey?" Jenny asked. "It's just a big ball of . . . something."

"Hold the towel," said Mrs. Hoade. "Dorothy, are you taking notes?"

"Yes, Mrs. Hoade."

"Okay," said Mrs. Hoade. "Now hold it up like this. That's it. Twist the end. That's right."

"It's getting heavy, Mom," said Lisa. The girls held the suspended turkey between them like a jump rope.

"Now swing it!" Mrs. Hoade instructed.

"Wrap string around circumference," Dorothy read aloud, "in several places to prevent slippage during cooking."

After the turkey had been rewrapped in the towel and held, this time by Mrs. Hoade at one end and Dorothy at the other, while Jenny tied the string around the middle, Dorothy wrote: *Two adults needed to hold turkey while the string goes around. Do not let turkey fall.*

"Now," said Mrs. Hoade, placing the bundle gently in the large baking pan of broth. "We need a weight, don't we?"

Dorothy checked the Gallantine recipe. "Yes," she said. "About ten pounds."

"How about that iron pot up there?" Jenny suggested.

"That's an antique," said Mrs. Hoade.

"There's half a cinder block outside the kitchen door," Dorothy said. "I could go get it and wrap another wet towel around it."

"Good thinking," said Mrs. Hoade.

First Dorothy wrote down *Cinder block (half) or other weight.*

Dorothy, Mrs. Hoade, Jenny, and Lisa all took one final look before they closed the oven door.

"Is it supposed to be that flat?" Lisa asked.

"Yes," said Mrs. Hoade.

The girls were permitted to stay up and watch *Dragnet*, in honor of this, the last recipe. Dorothy was asked if she would have a little celebration drink. Mrs. Hoade washed her hands, removed her apron, and ushered Dorothy into the living room. She sat down in her favorite chair, a wing-back covered with plum-colored velvet, next to a brass whaler's lamp. She poured herself a Scotch on ice. "Now tell me what's wrong with your sister," she said. "You were so upset before."

Dorothy settled herself on the sofa, her hands between her knees. "Oh, it's really nothing," she explained. "She wants me to go home Labor Day. That's not what bothered me. She thinks my riding is a bad thing to do."

"A bad thing to do! But you enjoy it so. Didn't you have a good ride today?"

"Oh, *yes*. It was the most perfect day of the summer. We went back to . . ." Dorothy stopped herself. "An old apple orchard," she invented on the spur of the moment.

"You must have a drink. You must keep me company," said Mrs. Hoade. "Get yourself a glass." Mrs. Hoade walked, a little unsteadily, over to the liquor tray. Reluctantly Dorothy roused herself to fetch a glass from the kitchen. She wished she could have shared the day's lovely experience with Mrs. Hoade. The sky had been bright blue, without a suggestion of haze. The air was dry and nearly cool. The birds had sung all over the woods like a chorus in a great leafy cathedral. She and Baldy had returned to the little Coburg graveyard. There a new grave, with a haze of baby-green grass upon it, marked Miriam Coburg, had taken its place among other members of its family. Again, Baldy had said that it ought to have been creepy. Dorothy's gaze had fastened on all the other peaceful old stones and crosses, some so vine-covered that the names were illegible, some so old that even if the latest Coburg to pass had lived to a hundred and ten, she couldn't possibly have known the ancestors who'd gone a century before. Whoever rested there, Dorothy had decided, rested, as the saying went, in peace, also in dignity and privacy. Her own Uncle Dennis had been buried in the St. James churchyard in Newburgh, she had told Baldy, "with strangers all around."

Dorothy congratulated herself on her tact, as she brought an old-fashioned glass in from the kitchen. To mention the graveyard, no matter how beautiful it was, might have saddened Mrs. Hoade.

"No. That's the wrong kind of glass for wine," Mrs. Hoade said. "You'll want an aperitif glass." She fetched a gold-chased sherry glass from another cabinet. Pouring out some very dark red liquor, she told Dorothy, "Now this is only blackberry wine. It won't hurt you and you ought to learn to drink properly. If you don't start with something light now, you'll be a drunk by the time you're twenty-one. Now tell me. Is it money you're worried about? I heard you tell your sister about the boots Baldy gave you. Something about paying for them?"

"No, it isn't money," said Dorothy, hoping to get off the topic of the riding boots. "The money is all set. I have to put it all in the bank anyway for my college education."

"What?" asked Mrs. Hoade. "Do you mean to tell me you've worked this hard all summer and you won't have a nickel to yourself?"

"I guess not," answered Dorothy. "But it's all right. After all, college is expensive. My parents have paid for my food and clothing all my life. I have to contribute if I can."

Mrs. Hoade swizzled the ice in her drink with her finger. "I have a surprise for you, Dorothy," she said.

"Yes?" Dorothy tried to block out all the possibilities that flooded to mind.

"I'm certainly going to acknowledge your contribution to the book, in print. I also think you deserve an extra hundred dollars for your work. In light of what you just told me, I'll make it a hundred and fifty."

"Oh, Mrs. Hoade, I couldn't. Thank you so much. But I just *couldn't*!"

"Why on earth not?"

"Well, first of all, it wouldn't be right. The time I spent on the cookbook was time I would have been watching Jenny and Lisa instead of them being up with the TV. So it isn't really extra work, it's just different work. The other thing is, my mother would make me send it back."

"Don't tell her!"

"Don't tell her? I've never . . . *not* told my mother anything in my life!"

Mrs. Hoade laughed. "I'll think of a way," she said. "In the meantime here's a toast to *In an Amish Kitchen.*"

Dorothy raised her glass and touched Mrs. Hoade's with it. She accepted a cigarette that Mrs. Hoade offered. She allowed Mrs. Hoade to light it for her and inhaled the smoke tentatively with a large swallow of the blackberry wine.

"I've changed the title, as you see," Mrs. Hoade went on. "I'll tell you why. . . ."

The wine and the tobacco and the stuffiness of the room began to mesmerize Dorothy. Matthew had forgotten to turn off one of his lawn sprinklers outside in the garden. It threw a shower of water against the window behind Mrs. Hoade every three seconds or so. The light from the whaler's lamp made the drops diamond bright. There was something about the wine that stirred a memory in Dorothy. She tried desperately to concentrate on what Mrs. Hoade was saying, but she kept picturing her Aunt Ruth. Her Aunt Ruth's parlor on Sunday afternoons. That was where she'd tasted blackberry wine before.

Tiny prisms of light rolled down the windowpane, only to be whipped aside as new drops took their place. Two nameless things began to merge in Dorothy's mind as if two ends of a rope were inexorably knotting themselves together in as perfect a clove hitch as one of Baldy's tethers. It began with a smell. The smell of

Aunt Ruth's parlor. Identical to the smell inside the cottage, when Miss Borg had opened the door the day Dorothy was looking for Lisa. The smell of lavender sachet in the bureau drawer. That was what I was looking for. It wasn't a thing at all. It was the smell that brought me back there. Dorothy shuddered.

"And then again," Mrs. Hoade was saying, "I had another idea for a title. Let me try this out on you."

"Yes?" said Dorothy. As surely as she knew the peculiar odor of Maureen's house—sometimes pleasant and powdery, usually sour and ammoniac—and the smell of every other house she'd been in that contained a baby, she knew for certain there had never been a baby in that cottage at all. Someone else had been kept there.

All the thoughts she had so successfully prevented herself from thinking during the past two weeks came rushing back to her. She couldn't stop them. What were the Hoades hiding? Whom had she seen in that window during the storm? What had happened to Miss Borg? Dorothy had not seen her come back from the hospital with Mr. and Mrs. Hoade. She had not gone to the burial. She had vanished.

Dorothy's glass dropped and shattered between her feet. "I'm a little sick, I think!" she said to a bewildered Mrs. Hoade. She dashed upstairs.

Dorothy hung her head out her bedroom window. She was determined not to be nauseated. She took several deep drafts of the crisp night air. Where was Miss Borg? Who was Miss Borg, anyway? Like an imp whispering in her ear, Mr. Hoade's voice repeated, "Borg is hardly in a position to bring anything out now." Somewhere beneath her, among the flowers and long pulverized by the rain, was a shred of paper that had said "witnes."

"Dorothy who?"

"Dorothy Coughlin, Sister. In second period English? I'm sorry to bother you, but . . ."

"Dorothy Coughlin! It's seven o'clock in the morning!"

"I know, Sister Elizabeth, but I thought you got up at six thirty."

"I do! But that doesn't make this hour of the day any more palatable for conversation. A nun is no better before her morning coffee than anyone else! Why on earth are you calling me, child? Where are you?"

Dorothy took a deep breath. "I'm in Llewellyn, Pennsylvania, Sister. And I'm frightened. My parents are over in Ireland. My sister Maureen thinks I'm crazy and Terrance is somewhere playing football in a camp." Dorothy glanced nervously at the grandfather clock that stood in the far corner of the living room. Its peaceful ticking was the only sound in the house. She took the telephone around the back of the pantry, as far as the wire would stretch, and cupped her hand over the mouthpiece.

Sister Elizabeth listened in silence to Dorothy's hurried disjointed story. She interrupted only once to say, "That sounds just like Maureen," when Dorothy described that conversation.

"I probably left out the most important thing, Sister," Dorothy said in conclusion. "It would be just like me. But I think I have told you everything. Do you think I'm crazy, too? I don't know what to do. I'm frightened." Sister Elizabeth did not answer. "Sister? Sister Elizabeth? Are you still there? Are you mad at me?"

"I'm thinking," said Sister Elizabeth. At last she cleared her throat, as if, Dorothy could not help thinking, she were about to embark on Lady Macbeth's soliloquy, which was her favorite recitation. Instead, she asked, "You say you actually saw someone in the cottage?"

"Yes. I'm pretty sure. Yes."

"How sure?"

"Well, it was just for a second, but I did see him . . . her, whoever it was." Dorothy added, "I know it wasn't the nurse, Miss Borg. Miss Borg is short and squat."

"I believe I can say with certainty, Dorothy, although I'll look it up to be sure, that the labor union you mention, loathsome as its leadership is, was not the one connected with that dreadful affair last year. . . . You say there's a fresh grave not far from the house?"

"Yes, Sister."

"But the name is Coburg."

"Yes, Sister."

"And his name is Hoade and her maiden name was Krasilovsky?"

"Yes, Sister."

"Well then, I can tell you one thing. People don't go around using other people's graveyards for nefarious purposes. The Coburg family, after all, might not like it. Do something."

"Yes, Sister?"

"If there's a phone book there, look up Coburg. If there's a listing anywhere near your place you can be sure your nurse is not in the grave you saw."

Dorothy picked up the telephone directory. It was dog-eared and five years out of date. "Coburg," she muttered. "Coburg, Abel; Coburg, Gerald . . . there's lots. Here it is. Coburg, M., Route 8, Llewellyn. It can't be too far. We're on Route 8 too. Maybe it's that big old house way up the road behind the hedges."

"Most likely, Dorothy," said Sister. "Well that's out. The word *witness*, by the way, is used on hundreds of kinds of mundane documents. You'll find it on marriage licenses, deeds, bills of attainder, wills, contracts of all kinds, mortgage agreements, IOUs, and even some foreign passports. There is no reason, in my opinion, to jump to the conclusion that a witness to that dreadful slaughter was being kept on the estate, and was—in your words, not mine, Dorothy—bumped off."

"Sister, I just have a feeling something's going on here."

"Well, if you're that frightened, I suggest you invent an excuse to come home. But I really doubt there is much amiss, Dorothy. These things simply don't happen to imaginative young girls. Only a very bad television program would come up with a drama like that." Sister Elizabeth pronounced the word television with the ac-cent on the third syllable, as if it were a brand-new invention. "Are you convinced, Dorothy? Are you no longer frightened?"

"I guess not, Sister. I mean, I guess I'm convinced."

Sister Elizabeth said nothing for a minute. Then her pause ended. "By virtue of your nose, you are positive a child was not in that house? And because you saw a grave that wasn't there two weeks ago, you are suspecting foul play?"

"Well, I don't know, Sister. I can't dig up the grave to see who's in it."

"Disinter, Dorothy. No, I'm sure there's a logical, aboveboard explanation for everything you've said. I'm afraid, however, that it mightn't be in your best interest to pursue this any further."

"You mean it's just plain none of my business, Sister?"

Sister laughed. "Exactly," she said. "I would not ordinarily admit this to a pupil, Dorothy, but I happen to be a devotee of Miss Agatha Christie. You see, even nuns have small vices. At any rate it's better than smoking cigarettes like Father Foley. So I admit to being intrigued by what you say. There is one thing in your story that doesn't fit in, but I cannot, for the earth, think what it is. I know it reminds me for some reason of the back of father's haberdashery store, when I was a little girl." Dorothy had never considered the possibility of Sister Elizabeth's ever being a little girl or having a father, much less one who ran a haberdashery, but then she had to have a father and he couldn't very well have been a Jesuit priest. She tried to stop herself thinking trivial things like that at a time like this. "I shall call you back,

Dorothy, if that something turns out to be of substance, or if I find your labor leader is a man in trouble. In the meantime, sit tight!"

Dorothy gave the number and hung up. She was positive she'd never heard the words *sit tight* spill from Sister's lips nor ever would again. There was a stirring and banging upstairs. Someone was getting up.

Dorothy stood at the bottom of the stairs. Mr. Hoade appeared suddenly at the top. "I didn't know you were here!" she blurted out.

"It's my house, isn't it?" he asked, coming down in his bathrobe. "I drove down late last night. You're up early."

"I was expecting a letter from my mother," Dorothy answered.

As if in answer to a prayer, Dorothy picked up the morning mail, which lay under the letter slot against the front door.

"A letter from my parents," she said with all the blameless youthful cheer she could muster. "And one from my best friend, Kate."

The hours until three o'clock dragged impossibly for Dorothy. Three was when Baldy would come around and pick her up. In the meantime Lisa had awoken with a cold and Mrs. Hoade with a hangover, and the turkey wouldn't make an aspic. When at last she swung herself into Charley's saddle, Dorothy felt quite out of sorts.

"Where do you want to go today?" Baldy asked.

"Back to the graveyard."

"Again? We went there yesterday."

"Tell you why later," said Dorothy. She remained uncommunicative as they trotted up a ridge, through the woods, and past the place where the farms in the valley could be seen in the splendor of their grain-filled fields. They passed over the wooden bridge exactly as they'd done the day before. Yesterday's hoofprints were still visible in the soft cinders on the other side of the bridge. The great nests of vines that they'd pulled up to read the headstones two weeks before had not fallen. This gave the little cemetery a disheveled look; Dorothy reminded herself to set them straight when she left this time.

"What are we looking for, Dorothy? Did you lose something?" Baldy wanted to know when they'd tied up their horses and dismounted.

"Something unusual. Something out of the ordinary," said Dorothy. She realized that she hadn't any idea what she was looking for.

"Like clues to a murder?" Baldy asked. "I've read some Nancy Drews. Tell me if we're looking for clues."

Dorothy laughed for the first time that day. "It sounds so silly, Baldy. It wouldn't help to explain it all. I'd rather not, because if I'm wrong it would be a cruel, awful rumor. So let's just go looking. Tell me if you see anything odd. Footprints, bits of cloth stuck to nettles, a pocket comb somebody dropped."

"Will you promise to tell me, if I find something?"

"Okay."

"Is it about the Hoades?"

"Yes," said Dorothy, feeling a little frightened and a little foolish all at once. She began examining the blackberry briars. Baldy followed at a respectful distance, eating an occasional berry when Dorothy wasn't looking.

If there had been any scraps of cloth caught on bushes, or objects dropped from pockets, Dorothy decided she wouldn't know what to make of them anyway. The rain of the past week would have obscured any footprints, except theirs of the day before, and those were in evidence in great abundance.

Dorothy sighed. In mystery stories, detectives always came upon things suspiciously left in graveyards. From a single heel mark Perry Mason, or even Della Street, could tell the identity of the wearer and whether he or she had been running, limping, or dragging a body.

"Well, we haven't found anything, have we?" Baldy asked at last, scratching her nose. "Will you tell me anyway, Dorothy?"

"Well, okay," Dorothy answered. "This is going to sound pretty dumb. Do you remember when I told you the baby had died? The Hoades' baby?"

"And so," said Baldy when Dorothy had finished the whole story, "you thought maybe a witness to that labor union murder was buried here?"

"I wondered. But I guess everything's on the up-and-up."

"If my uncle were home, he'd tell us right away about

this Coburg family. Probably knows the Hoades too. I could write him," she added helpfully.

"Takes too long," said Dorothy.

"Anyway," said Baldy, placing her left foot in Gabriel's stirrup and pulling herself into the saddle, "it's a cinch the Hoades never used this place to bury anybody. First of all the grave's too big to be a baby's. Secondly they wouldn't dare use someone else's property, if there are live Coburgs in the phone book."

Up and down, Baldy's compact, chunky form rose and fell as she posted with the precision of a Swiss clock. Gabriel trotted swiftly, almost soundlessly over the soft earth ahead of Dorothy and Charley. The sweat poured down Charley's neck like rain on a window. Dorothy flicked at it with her fingers, but it kept pouring down. Like the rain on the end of the coffin . . . "Oh Baldy!" Dorothy shouted. She felt her foot slip in the stirrup. "That's it!"

Baldy whirled around and pulled Gabriel up. "What's it? Do you want to give me a heart attack?" she asked.

"The coffin!"

"What coffin?"

"The coffin. The baby's coffin. It was so long that it took up the whole back of Matthew's station wagon. It wasn't a baby's coffin at all. There must have been a grown-up in it." Flies began to gather on Charley's ears. He wanted to get started again. Dorothy brushed them away. Why didn't Baldy say anything? Why was she so still, all of a piece with Gabriel like a civil war statue?

"I think you better stop, Dorothy," she said at last.

"Stop what?" Dorothy asked, wiping her face on her shirt sleeve.

Baldy had brought her horse up even with Charley's neck. Dorothy felt Baldy's strong warm hand play against her own wrist and hold it tightly. "Don't do this, Dorothy. Leave other people's skeletons in other people's closets. I know I'm not smart like you, but I do know one thing. I wouldn't mess around with that Mr. Hoade. Not for a million bucks. If there's anything you're not supposed to know about you better not find it out. Please!" Baldy paused for breath. "We've had such a wonderful time riding. I don't have any friends here, you know. I just want to look forward to what's left of the summer."

"You're right, Baldy," Dorothy said. "Maybe if I had Ned Nickerson to protect me it would be okay, but I don't."

"Who's he?"

"Nancy Drew's big strong boyfriend."

And what a thing to give up, she told herself when they'd gotten out of the narrow path that attracted so many horseflies. They cantered all the way to the top of a hill where Baldy said the view was most spectacular. If I meddle any further in this, Dorothy reasoned, I'll be fired and packed off home in a big fat hurry. There's not quite two weeks 'til Labor Day. Maybe Mrs. Hoade will let me ride more days instead of paying me extra money. She's sending the cookbook off to the publisher today. She can afford the time and so can I.

The goldenrod brushed against Charley's legs and under the bottoms of Dorothy's boots. At the top of the hill the wind blew, the horses ceased to sweat, and Dorothy pulled her hair back, as it had been plastered to her face with perspiration. "When it's not so hazy you can see five or six miles," Baldy told her. The view of the undulating pastures and oblong meadows full of field corn held Dorothy and Baldy speechless on their standing horses for a moment. Then Dorothy sighed and said, "I wish it were all mine, too."

"Yours, too? It doesn't belong to me or even to my uncle," Baldy said in surprise.

"Oh, yes, it does," said Dorothy.

Dinna had not taken home the pancake-shaped turkey, Mrs. Hoade informed Dorothy when Dorothy came in. However, she had decided to include the recipe in the package anyway. It was now in the mail, Mrs. Hoade went on to say with a positive twinkle in her eyes. There had been a call from Dorothy's sister, Mrs. Hoade added.

Dorothy pulled off her boots in the kitchen. She groaned. "Maureen? I wonder what she wants now. I hope Mom and Dad are okay."

"I expect they are," said Mrs. Hoade. "Dinna took the message." She peered at the greasy slip of paper with the dreadful handwriting. "Everything is hunky-dory. E.M.O.S.H.," she read, "that makes no sense. Must be a misspelling. Well, it doesn't seem to be much of an emergency. Now, get the girls washed up. We'll have turkey croquettes tonight, dear," said Mrs. Hoade, downing the rest of a large Scotch and pouring herself another.

Dorothy frowned at the telephone message as she climbed the stairs. Emosh? She smiled. Of course it wasn't Maureen. E.M.O.S.H. Elizabeth MacIntosh, Order of the Sacred Heart. If Dorothy hadn't known it was impossible, she would have imagined Sister was having fun with gangster movie words like hunky-dory and sit tight and her own encoded initials.

Mr. Hoade was changing his shirt in his bedroom as Dorothy went by. "Get your message?" he asked as he buttoned the third button down.

Dorothy shivered a little at his voice. "Yes, Mr. Hoade," she answered.

"I happened to pick up the extension at the pool," he said smoothly, "same time as Dinna picked it up in the kitchen." He looked at himself in the mirror for an instant. "Dinna thought it was your sister, but it wasn't. It was a nun, wasn't it?"

Dorothy crumpled the paper in her hand. She hoped Sister Elizabeth had said nothing more than hunky-dory. "Yes, my English teacher," Dorothy managed to stutter.

"Oh," said Mr. Hoade. He closed the door softly in Dorothy's face. "You don't mind? I'm changing my pants," he said, with a chuckle that Dorothy didn't particularly like.

"Time to get washed up for supper, girls!" Dorothy called into the library. "Mom says just a few minutes."

"Uhm" was the reply. It would, of course, be at least

an hour before Mrs. Hoade had anything ready. The girls seemed to know this as well as Dorothy. I have time to write to Kate, she thought. Poor Kate must think I'm dead. I haven't had a chance to write for the whole summer.

Dear Katey, she began, *I've been so busy every second that I haven't had a minute to write (or do much summer reading either).* Dorothy stared out her bedroom window into the leaves of the oak tree that stood outside. How far away Kate seemed to be from this spot. *I've been helping the lady I work for write a cookbook. You won't believe it but even I am a little more organized than she is. My name is going to go into it in print. Won't that knock Sister Elizabeth out!* Surely Sister had not said much more than hunky-dory. Surely Mr. Hoade had overheard nothing. Why would Sister even mention a labor union to Dinna? *You won't believe this either but these people have the most fabulous parties. Every week I have to order at least two hundred bucks worth of food and booze over the phone. I've never seen a hundred dollar bill before. I've actually paid out one or two hundred every time the caterer delivers, because Mrs. H. doesn't trust the maid with the change.* Why would he show such interest in a silly phone call? Particularly if everything was hunky-dory, as Sister had said. I'll just have to find a way of calling Sister back. All the phones are on this one line though. *The best thing about the whole summer is riding horseback. ME! The girl I ride with is very rich. She owns a horse. Can you imagine! We go all over the countryside, which is gorgeous. Even more beautiful than the Catskills.* The simple explanation for them using such a big coffin is that they probably couldn't get a little one this far out in the country. *You'll never guess who your best buddy met last week at one of the parties. Desi Arnaz! He's a gambling friend of Mr. H. I don't like Mr. H. one bit. He gives me the creeps.* The reason I was told not to go out to the cottage is that the surrounding area is full of rotting timbers, rusty nails, and snakes. *You remember how we always talked about marrying millionaires and having dinner in the Waldorf Astoria? Well, these people have all the money in the world. This lady did just that. I can tell. She married for money and wait 'til I tell you how that works out. Of course it would be different with David Niven or somebody.* But there really aren't any rotting timbers, rusty bits of iron, or snakes down there. There's only a fairly substantial cellar. *Anyhow, tell you all in September. Take care of yourself. Love, Dot.* Sister Elizabeth was much too smart to let the cat out of the bag on the telephone. Dorothy folded the letter and licked the envelope. No, there was just nothing to worry about.

Of course Dorothy was hot and tired after she had done all that big pile of dishes. Mrs. Hoade had used every pot and pan in the kitchen again to make her turkey croquettes. She didn't mind in the least if Dorothy went out to the mailbox on Route 8 to post her letter, and if she took a swim on the way back. Mrs. Hoade seemed unusually preoccupied that evening; perhaps with no guests and only Mr. Hoade to contend with, she was not very happy. At nine o'clock, Dorothy dried the last dish, changed into her bathing suit, and letter in hand walked down the driveway to the road.

She could see only the bulky shape of the cottage, a square of blackness, blacker than the woods that surrounded it. If they hadn't turned off the telephone down there, the call to Sister Elizabeth would be easy. Mrs. Hoade had never buzzed the phone in the cottage, she'd given the number to the operator. That meant a separate line.

Dorothy felt for the door handle. She gave the door a push as she depressed the latch. It opened so easily that she nearly tumbled in upon the door. The darkness in the little house surrounded her like a muff. Holding on to the wall with one hand, she rotated the other in wobbly circles to find a telephone, or at least a light switch. A light would not be seen at the big house, as the windows had been shuttered over on that side. Her fingers touched the top of a silk lampshade. She steadied it. Then the palm of her hand came directly on the soft lips of a human mouth.

Chapter

Eight

Dorothy found herself grasping the side of Miss Borg's bed, kneeling and then crouching beside it as if the walls at any moment might cave in around her. When Miss Borg had shouted whatever she was shouting in German for the third time, Dorothy managed to open her eyes and say, "I'm so sorry, Miss Borg. I didn't know you were still here. Please, I'm so sorry."

"*Was machst du hier?*" Miss Borg repeated. She hoisted herself upright against her pillow and began fussing with her hair. She used little bits of colored cloth as curlers, Dorothy noticed, and she wore a winter nightgown of white flannel. Some of the fright had left

Miss Borg's eyes. "*Gott im Himmel!*" she said in a grumpy voice.

"I'll go right now, Miss Borg," said Dorothy, pulling herself up to a standing position. She was about to back out the door when Miss Borg kicked aside her covers and strode over to the kitchen asking, "*Etwas Kaffee?*"

That sounded like coffee. Dorothy reckoned she'd better sit down and accept some hospitality, or Miss Borg, whatever her reason for staying on, might be further insulted and would be sure to tell Mrs. Hoade, perhaps Mr. Hoade.

"Yes, thank you," Dorothy answered, sitting on the bed. The kitchen was as tiny and efficient as a ship's galley. "*Was willst du von mir?*" Miss Borg asked, taking a small jar of Sanka from the shelf and putting a miniature kettle on to boil.

"Excuse me?" asked Dorothy.

"*Was willst du von mir? Was?*" Miss Borg asked again, more slowly.

Was was the word she'd used before, the day Dorothy had come down to the cottage in search of Lisa. Well, of course she must be wondering what I want, Dorothy reasoned. "I want to use the telephone," she said. "I want to call up a nun," she added, noticing that Miss Borg wore a small silver crucifix around her neck. "A nun . . . a"—What is the Latin for nun? Maybe she knows Latin—"*Nonna.*"

"*Nonne?*" asked Miss Borg, pointing to the cross around Dorothy's neck. "*Du wolltest mit einer Nonne telefonieren?*"

"May I make a telephone call to a convent?" Dorothy asked again. Miss Borg looked at her peculiarly. She motioned that Dorothy might use the telephone. Then she spooned two teaspoons of the coffee into the cups.

"Oh, thank you, so much," said Dorothy as earnestly as she could with as big a smile as she could manage. After a very long wait and several switchings of extensions, Sister's voice crackled through the receiver.

"I stayed up in the library, Dorothy," Sister said. "In case you called back. Everything's all right with your union, you know. Nothing to worry about."

"Thank you, Sister. You didn't say anything about unions over the phone this afternoon, by any chance?"

"Most certainly not. I know what an elementary precaution is, after all. So it seems your Mr. Hoade was only a bit crude. However, he was not lying."

"I guessed so, Sister. I found Miss Borg, by the way," Dorothy said with a smile at Miss Borg. Miss Borg smiled back with comprehension. "I'm right in the cottage now. She's making me a cup of coffee."

"Wonderful! So you see?" Sister laughed a little. "People aren't as awful as all that. We should remember to leave this sort of intrigue for the gothic writers. So it was a baby after all and the nurse is staying on until she finds another position?"

"That must be it, Sister. The nurse only speaks German so I can't really ask her."

"Deutsch," said Miss Borg pleasantly, stirring the coffee.

"A difficult language," Sister went on. "At any rate,

Dorothy, although I admit to being attracted to melodrama, I am relieved at what you say. I shouldn't want any of my students to come to a violent end."

"No, Sister," said Dorothy.

"However," Sister Elizabeth continued, "had you found yourself in a position that could have been described as unsavory, I'm sure you would have faced it with equanimity. An unsafe position you would have faced with courage. Any of my students would have done. 'Courage mounteth with occasion.' That's *King John.* You'll have it senior year."

"Yes, Sister."

"Was there anything else?"

"Not really, Sister. I didn't tell you that they buried the baby in an adult-size coffin. I guess they could only get a regular size one out here in the country. But there was something you said over the phone this morning, something that didn't fit in?"

"No doubt there's a mundane explanation for the coffin size," said Sister Elizabeth slowly. "No, this morning I was only thinking of a name. Your employer's maiden name. Krasilovsky. It reminded me of the back of my father's store. That's because he had a safe there, which he allowed me to open every morning before school. The brand name on the safe was Krasilovsky, and if you gave me a day I could probably remember the combination, as I did it every morning for seven years. Oh, dear. My memory is not what it was. At any rate, you are all right and whatever her name in the grave is, is resting in peace?"

"Miriam Coburg, Sister. Yes. And I'm going to enjoy the rest of the summer. Finishing *Nicholas Nickelby*, of course, and *Ivanhoe*." Dorothy could not hear Sister's reply to this statement. Miss Borg had dropped a coffee cup and was signaling furiously. "Excuse me, Sister, just a second, the nurse is very upset." Dorothy watched helplessly as Miss Borg rattled on in rapid German. "Please," she tried to interrupt, "I can't understand. Wait until I get off the phone."

"Dorothy, Dorothy," Sister called through the wire at the same time.

"Yes, Sister?"

"I cannot guarantee that the German I studied at Trinity College in Dublin twenty years ago will stand up, but perhaps I can reassure your friend, or understand what is happening."

Dorothy held the telephone out to Miss Borg, who with a great heaving sigh placed it against her ear. "She speaks German," Dorothy said to the doubt-filled blue eyes. The German did not slow down, nor did Miss Borg seem less agitated after ten or eleven minutes' talking to Sister Elizabeth.

"What is it? What's she upset about?" Dorothy asked when she was able, at last, to snatch the receiver back.

Sister sighed. "My German is really very elementary," she admitted sadly. "She's a Catholic."

"I know she's a Catholic."

"Nearly all German Catholics come from the south. Bavaria," Sister explained. "I'm sorry to say they are far more excitable and less methodical than their Prussian neighbors. Also, she uses a dialect."

"Oh," said Dorothy.

"I was only able to make out the last part where she slowed down a bit. The first part was all medical, I believe. She is apparently leaving to live with her sister in Munich. I suggest you ask her to write down, in an orderly fashion, whatever it is that is consuming her passion, and then translate it."

"But Sister, I don't know a word of German."

"Use a dictionary. Is there one handy? Use your considerable gift for languages."

"Yes, Sister, but . . ."

"Dorothy, one day you will find yourself at a very fine university. You will have to read Goethe and Schiller. So you might as well start now. There's no sense in reading Goethe and Schiller in English. Can you imagine how ludicrous Sir Walter Scott would be in German? I will see you in September and you'll show me the results of your efforts?"

Dorothy glanced over at Miss Borg. The nurse was still talking, still explaining in German, now to no one. Her voice, under the impossible-sounding guttural syllables, was as crushed as a frightened child's.

"I'll do it, Sister," said Dorothy. "Poor Miss Borg is upset. Even if I don't get a word, maybe it'll make her feel better, anyhow."

There was a very short pause at the other end of the wire. Dorothy thought perhaps the line had gone dead. "God bless you, Dorothy," said Sister, never for an instant losing the crispness in her tone. "I think you'll find your way."

Dorothy hung up without being able to reply. Nobody save her parents had ever said "God bless you" to her before, certainly not a teacher. How funny teachers could be outside the classroom. They actually seemed to have lives and feelings like real people.

The coffee was lukewarm. Dorothy scanned the bookshelf. Her eye came to rest on the small German dictionary that Miss Borg had brought with her on their walks among the flowers. She removed it from the shelf and, taking a writing tablet and pencil from the bureau, indicated to Miss Borg that she should write down what she was trying to communicate.

Miss Borg wrote. She crossed out and rewrote furiously. Dorothy watched her, dictionary in hand, and thought about Sister Elizabeth. Surely Sister knew about her upcoming punishment for what had happened at the Assembly. The whole school knew about it. Sister Elizabeth must have been just as shocked as Reverend Mother. Maybe, Dorothy thought, looking through the pages of German words, this will be much tougher than taking the Latin exam over again, even if no one gives me a grade on it. I'll do the best I can, she decided, even if I'm not interested in what this poor old lady is upset about. I guess I'd rather die than let Sister down.

Dorothy's interest in what the poor old lady had to say was sharpened the minute she looked at Miss Borg's block letters. There was not a single word on the whole paper that resembled any Latin, any French, not to mention English, save one, and that was *Autopsie*. Dorothy smoothed out a sheet of paper from the writing tablet. She drew horizontal lines on it. "I can't think without lined paper," she said to Miss Borg. No recognition appeared in Miss Borg's face. I'll just pretend it's like a French exam, Dorothy decided. I'll translate the big words to get the gist of it and try to fill in the little ones and the grammar later. If I have time, she added to herself, looking at the clock.

Ich bin eine gute Christin und eine gute Kranken-schwester. I something something Christian and nurse? Yes. "*Gute Christin*," Miss Borg was saying. It certainly sounded like "Good Christian." All right. She was a good Christian and a good nurse. *Ich habe nichts Schlechtes getan. Die nächtlichen Besuche waren schlecht. Das Kreischen und das Anschreien waren schlecht. Außerdem war es eine Sünde, etwas ganz Schreckliches* . . . Awful! Dorothy thought. She stared at the sentence. On the other hand there was a word repeated several times. *Schlecht*. She pointed to it and Miss Borg looked it up for her. "*Ja*," said Miss Borg. Wrong, bad, it turned out to be. Miss Borg indicated the second sentence. *Ich habe nichts*, that was the key. *Nichts* was nothing. *Ich* was I. *Getan*, probably done. I have done nothing bad. Okay. What was bad, or wrong? The *Kreischen*, shouting and *Anschreien*, shrieking? yelling? Keep going, Dorothy, Dorothy reminded herself. . . . *überhaupt jemand in dieser Hütte*—something in this cottage. "*Schlecht*," Miss Borg said emphatically, tapping a pen at this particular sentence—*gegen ihren*

Willen zu halten. Willen was intent or will, *halten* was stop or hold, yes, and *Hütte*, like hut, was cottage. Dorothy looked at what she'd now translated. The good Christian and nurse, the bad shouting and yelling and now this. A guess, but maybe it would come clear later. Kept in here against her will. Well, a young baby wouldn't care where it was kept. This must mean Mrs. Hoade did not approve of the baby's being stashed away in the cottage. She hurried down the page.

Das Einzige, was ich getan habe, war Medizin zu enhalten, die ihr Leiden verlängerte. A better sentence. Two words to look up. *Leiden* and *verlängerte*. Suffering and prolong. The medicine was halted and the suffering prolonged? Come back to this. Dorothy made a small asterisk. *Sie nahm massige Dosen ein.* Something about massive doses. The German grammar was unfathomable to her. At least, however, most of the important words, the ones Miss Borg kept pointing to and looking up for her, were capitalized. *Sie wollten ihr Leben natürlich solange wie moglich verlängern, selbst wenn es sich nur um ein paar Tage handeln sollte.* Something about wanting to prolong her life again. *Der Arzt*, that meant doctor, *behauptete, das neue Medikament*, something this new medicine, *würde ihr Leben um 48 Stunden verlängern*—the doctor something this new medicine prolong her life by 48 hours. Getting somewhere, now, Dorothy thought—*aber ich konnte mich nicht dazu bringen, ihr noch eine schmerzhafte Spritze zu geben.* Miss Borg was now making plain gestures. Her two fingers and thumb worked an invisible hypodermic. She indicated an enormous needle. Then she grimaced horribly, shaking her head, and pointed to the paper again. I can (could?) myself not bring to something these horrible injections. So that was the "medicine halted." Miss Borg could not bring herself to give another painful dose of the medicine. Dorothy winced. And with only forty-eight hours for the poor little baby to live, at the most. Well, of course not. What an awful word *Spritze* was for an injection. *Sie weinte immer und sträubte sich so dagegen.* How awful. Something about struggling and crying against it. But here was the interesting part about the autopsy coming up. *Anstatt noch ein oder zwei Tage länger zu leben, starb sie in Frieden.* Instead, that even sounded like *Anstatt*. Something about a day longer, died in freedom, not in peace. Now. Here it was. *All dies kann natürlich leicht bewiesen werden. Bewiesen* —shown by evidence or proof. *Die Autopsie wird aufzeigen, daß die verschriebene Medizin nicht gegeben war.* Dorothy looked up at Miss Borg's very agitated face. She understood, after looking up just a few words. The autopsy was written down. A copy of it would prove that the prescribed medicine had not been given. "You could be in trouble," she said to Miss Borg. Miss Borg looked at her uncomprehendingly. She pointed to another sentence. *Kein anständiger Mensch könnte das laute Anschreien*—something about loud angry shrieking—*aushalten*—endure—*wenn sie abends herüber kam.* No decent person angershrieking endure when something here came, came over here.

Herr Hoade—aha! said Dorothy. So there it is. What

does she say about him? The word angershrieking seemed to fit him well—*hat meine Rückfahrt nach Deutschland bezahlt und mir eine Menge Geld gegeben.* Mr. Hoade has return passage to Germany paid and a lot of gold? The same word, *Geld*, meant money. *Ich wollte das Geld nicht, aber von irgend etwas muß ich ja leben. Ich habe nichts geerbt und nicht veil gespart.* I didn't want the gold, no, money and then something about no inheritance and no savings. Dorothy guessed that Miss Borg had been forced, somehow, by her own straitened circumstances to accept money from the Hoades. Well, at least she was going back to Germany. Sister Elizabeth had found that out too. Dorothy peered at the clock. She would have to run in a couple of minutes. Her pencil paused over the part she had just translated. I wonder why Mr. Hoade wanted to pay her and send her back home, Dorothy mused. Miss Borg seemed to notice Dorothy's hand, which was now doodling slightly around the word *Geld*. She opened her bureau drawer and produced both a steamship ticket for the *Bremen* and a cashier's check for the sum of $10,000. This seemed to confirm something for Miss Borg. She was nodding as if Dorothy had asked her to prove the validity of the sentence.

Dorothy looked at the bottom of the page; all that remained was a reassertion of the good Christian, and good nurse, and a plea that the *heilige Jungfrau*, holy young lady? no, Blessed Virgin, forgive her if she'd done wrong.

Without all the little words, the pronouns, the conjunctions, and connectives, Dorothy couldn't be exactly sure of her translation. It would take forever to look them up. This much was clear to her. The baby had been kept in the cottage against Mrs. Hoade's will. Mr. Hoade had come down—*herüber* was apparently the German for "come hereover"—and had yelling fits for some reason, and Miss Borg had felt so sorry for the poor little thing that she'd allowed her to die peacefully. If the Hoades had a German dictionary up at the house, perhaps she'd be able to look up some of the little words and make more sense of the paper. *Es, sie, wenn. Es,* she made a note, after finding it, meant it and also there is. Capitalized it meant the musical E flat. Impossible! Dorothy said to herself. *Sie* meant they, you, she . . . did it mean if, as well? No, that was the French *si.* At least Latin made some sense in its consistency. At least in French there were recognizable words. The Germans seemed to string all manner of words together to make single big words. Like *Anschreien.* A noun meaning shrieking-at in English. Still, Dorothy had to admit it had a ring to it. Shrieking at a girl baby, a sick one at that. What an appropriate word for Mr. Hoade's way of speaking. The quiet voice that, when it didn't get what it wanted, became too quickly a yell, like a shove.

"I don't understand all of this now," she said to Miss Borg. She took up the dictionary again. "Not . . . *nicht verstehen* . . ." She looked up everything in the English half. "*Alles.* But . . . *mais* . . . no, that's French. I won't say a word!" She put her finger to her lips, and crossed her heart with her other hand.

"*Ja?*" asked Miss Borg, color coming back into her face for the first time in half an hour.

"*Guten* . . ." What is it? "*Abend. Guten Abend,*" said Dorothy.

"*Gute Nacht, danke schön,*" said Miss Borg, and she took Dorothy's hand in hers and, smiling over whatever German she decided not to say, pressed it with great warmth.

There was no German dictionary in the library upstairs. The girls were in bed, sleeping in two little hunched-up bundles of sheets. Dorothy waited a moment in their doorway to make sure they were all right. Jenny moved and sighed. Lisa's thumb was thrust securely in her mouth. Dorothy closed the door.

The Hoades had gone to bed early too, it appeared from the snoring in the bedroom. She wandered around the empty living room looking at the bookshelves. No German dictionary. She'd have to wait and finish her translation at the Newburgh Public Library. In the meantime, Miss Borg's paper and her translation were safely squirreled away in the spine of her *Ivanhoe* upstairs. The Hoades did have a complete set of Shakespeare, however, bound in blue morocco leather. Courage mounteth with occasion, she said to herself and pulled out *King John*. This ought to put me to sleep in a hurry, Dorothy decided, collapsing full length on the sofa. She yawned at the characters in order of appearance.

The family photographs on the long mahogany table

in back of the sofa all faced her. They gave the appearance of intruding. Dorothy tried to read *King John*.
"Went down over Pearl Harbor. Pearl Harbor bomb-
ing," she murmured to herself, looking uncomfortably
into the eyes of Mrs. Hoade's father. What a minimal
way to explain having your plane shot out of the sky.
This was a better picture of Mr. Krasilovsky than the
one in Mrs. Hoade's locket. Well, he was younger. This
was taken before the war and the other was taken in
1948.

Wait a minute. The war had been concluded in 1945.
Yet Dorothy was sure of the date in the locket. She'd
counted back eight years. A voice mewed in her head to
get reading, to concentrate on *King John*. Mrs. Hoade's
father never lived to see 1948, Dorothy told herself
calmly. And that probably wasn't his name at all, because
that obviously wasn't a date. It was . . . She tried
to remember the other numbers, but only the 48 had
stuck in her mind. It was a combination to a Krasilovsky
safe.

The lamplight played brilliantly through the cut-glass
angles at the throat of each decanter on the silver liquor
tray in the corner. It penetrated deeply into the various
liquors. Some were dark like the port, labeled in script
on a thin silver collar. Some were light like the vermouth,
as yellow as a cat's eye.

Above the tray hung the portrait. Dorothy looked
down at her wrist, still slightly scarred from Lisa's bite,
the evening she had crashed into it. She put *King John*

on the sofa. The painting had not moved from the wall, as a painting ought to do if it was normally hung up on a normal nail.

She touched the frame lightly, then a little less delicately. She slipped her fingers around the back of the right side. A catch gave and it swung away from the wall like a door.

The safe had been papered over, years ago, it seemed, for the wallpaper behind the painting was unfaded. Under a group of medieval musicians in the pattern Dorothy felt the recessed knob of the dial. She would have thought it was only a blank wall if she hadn't run her fingers carefully over it several times. Forty-eight, she thought. The rest of it is written on the back of that tiny picture, and Mrs. Hoade doesn't even know.

"I'll never know either," she whispered as she closed the painting. "Mrs. Hoade wears that locket every day."

The steady gaze of the woman above looked very nearly alive. The flowing dress, its sleeves eternally furled in a forgotten wind, the long fingers resting forever on the greyhound's head seemed about to move, but the longer Dorothy stared at it, the more solid it became, as if the woman in the picture had decided at the last moment not to say anything.

"Who are you?" Dorothy asked aloud. "Are you Katherine Hoade? Where are you now?"

Coburg, Abel; Coburg, Gerald; Coburg, M.—"Llewellyn three oh five eight four," Dorothy said to the operator.

Busy signal. Well, that's that, Dorothy told herself.

There *are* Coburgs. Katherine Hoade wouldn't be buried in that grave. Neither would her great-granddaughter. Dorothy gave the number one more time to the operator.

"Miss?" asked the operator.

"Yes?" said Dorothy.

"You are calling a wrong number. I suggest you look up your party's correct listing in the telephone directory."

"But I did," said Dorothy, her index finger resting on the number before her. "Maybe the telephone book misprinted it."

The operator paused. Then she said, "The telephone book has no misprints, Miss. You are calling your own number."

Chapter

Nine

"I wish you hadn't asked the kids to come with us," whispered Dorothy, rebuckling the strap of her left stirrup.

"Oh, but they'll have fun," Baldy answered. "Look at Lisa now, she's trotting so prettily. It isn't fair to just make them ride in the ring. They should be rewarded for how well they've both learned with a nice ride through the woods."

"But I wanted to talk to you."

"What about?" Baldy asked warily, leaning over from Gabriel's back and helping Dorothy find the right notch.

"I got the combination. Last night Mrs. Hoade called

me into the bathroom while she was taking a shower. The locket was lying right there."

"Dorothy," said Baldy, straightening up in her saddle, "I don't want to hear about it. Lisa!" she shouted. "Don't go over that log. Your mom says no jumping yet. Go ahead now, Jenny. Your turn. Walk and trot three times around, then we'll go up the hill." Jenny guided her pony, Texas, in a slow circle in the open pasture. "Lisa!" Baldy called. "Hold your horse right there. I want to see you rein him in. He shouldn't follow Texas unless you want him to." Amazing, Dorothy thought, they do everything Baldy asks them to.

"It's a cinch the silly safe is empty if it's been papered over, anyway," said Baldy. "Dorothy, this is your last day. Won't you just enjoy it and forget that other business?"

Charley stamped in the powdery brown earth. Dorothy pulled him back and lowered her voice so the girls couldn't hear. "All I want to know," she said, "is why this Miriam Coburg, who died around the same time as the Hoades' baby, lived in the Hoades' cottage. She must have been the person I saw in the window that night. Who was she?"

Baldy rolled her eyes and looked heavenward. "This is the very last thing I'm going to say on that subject," she announced. "Then we'll drop it." She inhaled deeply. "Supposing, as you said, the kid was never in the little house at all. Supposing the kid is the Katherine Hoade in—where is it? Crestview? Okay. Supposing the nurse was taking care of his grandmother the whole time. For some reason they just didn't want you and Lisa and Jenny to be around a sick old lady. Maybe she was crazy. I don't know. People have reasons for things. That doesn't mean there was a crime or anything."

"But the name, Baldy. Her name was Coburg, not Hoade."

"Well, it could be his mother's mother, couldn't it? Then the name would have had to be different."

"I never thought of that," Dorothy admitted.

"All I've heard so far," said Baldy, "is that you were told a convenient lie. It's their business, Dorothy. It isn't yours. Now promise me something."

"Depends what it is."

"Promise me you'll go out to dinner with the Hoades tonight and then take the train, everything as planned. Promise me you won't go looking around in that wall."

"Baldy . . ."

"Mrs. Hoade asked you to come back next year, right?"

"Well, that's what she said. Unless the girls go to camp."

"And you're going to jeopardize that by being . . . well, by poking your nose where it doesn't belong."

"But Baldy, I . . ."

"Oh, Dorothy . . . I wish you wouldn't. I don't know how to say this, but I don't have many friends. Everybody at school thinks I'm fat and stupid. I promised Uncle I'd be here again next summer, because I thought—well, I was looking forward to riding with you again. It's so lonely otherwise."

"I'm sorry," said Dorothy.

"Then you promise?"

"Okay."

"Three times! Jenny," she shouted across the field. "At a trot. That's it. A little faster now, kick him. Make him do what you want, not what he wants to do!" Baldy looked with satisfaction at Jenny for a moment, then she turned to Dorothy. "I don't know how to say this," she began, "without sounding—what's the word? I can never remember. You know, looking down on someone as if I'm so great and all?"

"Patronizing?" Dorothy asked.

"That's it. Anyway, Dorothy, if you ask me, I mean there's nothing at all *wrong* with not being able to ride or not having any . . . much . . . a whole bunch of money and everything, but you've said how much you liked spending the summer here. You've said how different it is from anything you've done before, and I just think you should plan on Mrs. Hoade asking you back and not worry about silly invented things."

"Gee, you sound just like my sister, Maureen," said Dorothy.

"Well, I don't mean to. But first of all, as you've told me, you want to find a way someday not to have to be poor?"

"Yes?"

"Well, it seems to me you can start by meeting people and doing things and getting used to things that aren't . . . that are, you know, what you want, someday. And the other thing is, everybody has some awful events happening in their family. It isn't your business—whatever's gone on here. I mean you haven't exactly watched someone chop someone else up with a hatchet like Lizzie Borden, have you?"

"No," Dorothy admitted.

"Well, for heaven's sake leave well enough alone, then."

"I said I would," Dorothy answered.

Baldy urged Gabriel up the path. "I'm really very fond of you, Dorothy," she said mildly, over her shoulder. "Please come back next summer."

"Come on!" yelled Lisa to Jenny. "Let's go! You're slow as molasses."

"I'll take her," said Dorothy, grabbing Jenny's lead line. "Jenny and I will walk. You go trot and catch up with Baldy."

Maureen's voice insinuated itself in Dorothy's ear, through the rustling leaves and the *clop-clop* of the four horses' hooves. "Got yourself fired on the last day, eh?" it snipped. "Well you won't be going back there again, will you? You won't get your working papers 'til the year after next so I guess you'll have to spend next summer at the Veterans' Hospital." Oh, shut up, Dorothy mouthed to the air. "Serve you right," Maureen went on. "You can't even be grateful to people who are nice to you. Have to go prying into their stuff. I told you over the phone not to do that. I told you years ago not to go through *my* drawers, but I guess you didn't listen."

Here and there a tree or bush had begun to turn from bright green to soft yellow. The beginning of fall, of course, Dorothy thought. It'll be so lovely here. Not that I won't see trees turn all over Newburgh, and Sundays we go for a drive in the country sometimes, when Dad has off. Jenny and Dorothy plodded on in silence, the lead line dragging between them.

The goldenrod now filled almost every meadow they passed. Dorothy wished she would be able to see autumn here, to smell it and ride through it. I'll probably never have a chance to ride again, she thought sadly, unless next summer . . . Listen to Baldy, she told herself. For once listen to someone older and more sensible than you.

Mrs. Hoade looks just like a dog waiting for its master. Dorothy did not want to think that thought. She cleared her throat, announcing her presence. Mrs. Hoade had been seated on the living-room window seat, as usual, waiting for Mr. Hoade's rented Rolls to turn into the driveway. She was crying quietly.

"Excuse me," said Dorothy guiltily.

"Oh, dear. Did you have a nice ride?"

"Yes, beautiful."

"And the girls?"

"They loved it. Even Jenny. Lisa's in the tub. She was very dirty. Jenny's watching *Mr. Wizard*," Dorothy said. "I'll go."

"No, don't, dear. I want you to see this. I'm afraid there won't be too much of a celebration dinner tonight." Mrs. Hoade held out the crumpled package. Several recipe cards fell on the carpet at her feet. Dorothy read the letter from the publisher.

Dear Mrs. Hoage,

Mr. George Kebab is on vacation in Europe at this time. As you are no doubt aware, the Doubleday list is limited to a few hundred quality books a season. We find at this time that *The Amish Country Cookbook* does not meet our present needs. Another publisher may disagree however and we encourage you to try elsewhere. Thank you for sending us your manuscript, which we are returning herewith.

> Sincerely,
> Rhoda Gripper
> Editorial Assistant

"Well," Dorothy gulped, "it isn't all that bad, Mrs. Hoade."

"Look at the way they spelled my name!"

"Well," said Dorothy, sitting down heavily and picking up the pages that had fallen. Mrs. Hoade lit a cigarette and took a large swallow of her drink. "I think we could fix it," said Dorothy.

"Fix what?" Mrs. Hoade asked.

"For instance here. I think this is wrong. On the spoonbread recipe." Dorothy didn't dare say This is one of yours, not mine.

"Where, dear?"

"Well, it says half flour, half milk, half eggs."

"But that's exactly what Dinna put in."

"I don't think you can have three halves," said Dorothy.

"Why not? It's a delicious recipe. I saw her make it and I wrote down just exactly how she did it."

"Well, I think there are only two halves in a whole."

"I see what you're getting at," said Mrs. Hoade. "Perhaps if we . . . Well, you won't be here, but if I change those things and then when Mr. Kebab himself comes home instead of this stupid Gripper girl—it's probably just a big mistake. She can't even spell!"

Dorothy felt that somehow it wasn't a mistake, but she didn't want to say so. She nodded and smiled instead. Poor Mrs. Hoade. Poor Baldy, too. For an instant she looked over at the portrait. Twelve–six–forty-eight ran through her mind. "Mr. Hoade will be home any minute. Why don't you go up and get dressed? There he is," she said with evident pleasure. The Rolls crunched in the driveway and came to a halt. The door slammed. Dorothy watched Mr. Hoade for a moment. He did not acknowledge his wife's cheerful wave.

"I . . . uh . . . wanted to tell you I don't feel so hot," said Dorothy. "I thought I'd lie down. Can you and Mr. Hoade go?"

"You probably think it'll be a dreary evening, dear. I don't blame you."

"Oh, no, Mrs. Hoade." The front door opened. Mr. Hoade threw his briefcase on the sofa and loosened his tie. "Haven't you gotten dressed yet?" he asked. "We have reservations in an hour, I thought. I drove like crazy to get here."

Courage mounteth with occasion, said Dorothy to herself. "Mr. Hoade, I wasn't feeling too well and . . ."

"Does this mean it's off?" he asked. "Because I have work to do."

"I could make us some chicken," said Mrs. Hoade.

"No," said Mr. Hoade. "No. But if *she* isn't coming there's no sense going to the Carriage House in Bryn Mawr. We'll just go down the road to . . . that place, whatever it's called." He poured himself a drink and stood with it in his hand until Dorothy left the room. "What's wrong with her?" Dorothy heard him ask when she'd reached the upstairs hall.

"Dear, I don't know. I expect she might have a little tummy ache."

Dorothy shuddered. "Oh, for crying out loud," Mr. Hoade replied angrily.

I wonder if I'll be attacked in Grand Central Station, tonight. Dorothy asked herself as she lay on her bed. She figured she'd better lie down in case someone checked on her. Maureen had told her several times to get the early train from Philadelphia in order to get the last train out to Newburgh. Instead, Dorothy had chosen to go riding just one more time with Baldy. That meant she'd have to wait four hours in Grand Central Station for the morning milk-train home. "Go ahead," had been Maureen's parting shot yesterday morning over the phone. "So long as you're here by seven A.M. and we can leave for the beach. But don't blame me if some hobo comes up to you. If you see a policeman, stay nearby. Don't fall asleep on a bench or someone will come up and take your purse or maybe knife you." Dorothy punched her pillow. She pictured herself following a policeman around the station for four hours. She pictured herself going downstairs with a razor blade, one side protected by adhesive tape. Opening up the painting again. The girls would be watching television, of course. Other than Jenny and Lisa, the house would be empty. As she fell into a doze, Dorothy remembered about Mrs. Hoade's book. She'd been so disappointed for Mrs. Hoade that she'd hardly had time to feel disappointed herself. Her name wouldn't be in print, after all. Nothing to impress Sister Elizabeth with, after all. Well . . .

An empty house would have been too good to be true. Dinna, who had been asked to sit for the girls, had stayed on to finish some sewing. Dorothy stood in the darkened living room watching Dinna's broad back through the laundry-room door at the end of the pantry. Could I still be dreaming in bed? she asked herself. If I am, I'm definitely *not* going to do this when I wake up. You don't have to, she said reasonably to herself. There's still time to put the razor blade back. Take the tape off, go watch Sid Caesar with Jenny and Lisa, and forget about the whole thing.

The laundry-room door was closed. Through the glass Dinna could have a full view of Dorothy, standing at the foot of the stairway, opening the strongbox in the wall. On the other hand, she probably couldn't hear much. The window was thick.

She slid her hand around the back of the frame and released the tiny clasp. The blade went into the paper easily, at the outlines of the safe. Dorothy looked up. Dinna still sewed away. The red, raw arm lifted the

needle and fell to the cloth, something tweed, in a mes-
merizing rhythm. The single light in the laundry room
twinkled on Dinna's yellow hair. Dorothy pressed the
blade against the depressed circle around the knob. She
scraped away enough paper to free it. She couldn't see
the numbers.

She closed the painting again and walked over to the
chair that Mrs. Hoade favored. She turned on the
whaler's lamp. After a minute by the grandfather clock,
Dorothy sauntered back, her hands in her pockets. Dinna
had not turned around. She had not finished sewing.
Twelve–six–forty-eight, Dorothy repeated to herself. Is
it to the left first, the right? Am I supposed to listen for
clicks? Dinna's shoulders breathed heavily under her
flowered housedress in the pool of light in which she sat.
The metal door swung away, suddenly. Oh, dear Jesus,
bless me, said Dorothy. Dinna stopped sewing. She shook
out some threads from the tweed jacket she'd been
mending and turned around. She walked directly from
the laundry room through the pantry into the kitchen.
Dorothy sat in Mrs. Hoade's chair beside the whaler's
lamp. The safe and the painting were closed. In her
hands was a manila envelope. . . .

One more time, Dorothy got up and checked that the
door to her room was locked. She sat on the bed. The
shrill laughter from the television echoed down the hall.
Dorothy tossed the envelope onto her bureau, noticing as
she did that the handwriting on it looked familiar. WILL,
it said, in a hand identical to the numbers on the locket
picture. The same purple ink, as well.

I, Miriam Hess Coburg, it began. Dorothy listened for half a minute. No one was in the hall. She would have heard them come up on the creaking stairway.

Being of sound mind, the same flowing hand continued, *and in full awareness that this will, called holographic because it was prepared without the assistance of attorneys (whom I have no wish to consult) or the signature of witnesses (whom I have no wish to inform), is legal in the state of Pennsylvania and shall remain so after my death. I do bequeath all my worldly goods to be held in trust, for the benefit during her lifetime of my faithful friend and companion, Hilda Borg.* "Miss Borg!" said Dorothy in a whisper. "Miss Borg, you're rich!" She read quickly through to the end. The rest simply stated that when Miss Borg died the "worldly goods" would be held in trust for whatever great-grandchildren might be alive. They weren't to get the money until they had reached the "sensible age of thirty." It was signed and dated September 11, 1944. "Miss Borg!" said Dorothy again. She stuffed the will into her pocket. The Hoades had been gone over an hour and a half. How far was the restaurant? She still had a little time. Perhaps thirty minutes? So Katherine Hoade really was a baby and really was at Crestview. The bill proved that. She wiped her hand on her dungarees before touching the light switch. She could feel the sweat form again in the creases of her palm the minute the light was out.

"I left my bathing cap at the pool," Dorothy said to Jenny and Lisa. "I'm just going to get it."

"Uh huh," they both answered, not taking their eyes

off the gray-blue screen for a moment. Their hands popped in and out of a shared Crackerjack box like mechanical pincers on an assembly line.

"Don't swallow the prize," she advised them before she closed the door. The girls did not answer or seem to know she was gone. I think I'll always picture them like that, Dorothy thought, open mouths, open eyes, blue light not found in nature.

The sharp pebbles in the driveway abused the soles of her bare feet as she hopped over them. Dorothy cursed herself for forgetting her shoes. The raspberry runners around the cottage would hurt even more. The beginnings of a ground fog had gathered on the lawn. The dew soaked the cuffs of her dungarees and the cloth made an uncomfortable rim of cold around each ankle. As she ran across the grass her cross bounced up and struck her painfully in the teeth. Dorothy thought of finding Mrs. Hoade's wallet over three months ago, of hoping to be paid for a good deed. I really am just trying to do what I should, she thought. It's Miss Borg's money, and I'll just give her the will and be done with it. She searched her conscience. No, she certainly did not expect Miss Borg to reward her in any way. Perhaps she could finally believe that she was doing something just because it was right. What then was that newborn snake-in-the-grass at the back of her mind? Yes, of course. Dorothy Coughlin, Girl Detective. My, would Sister be pleased with her courage. Would they have a special assembly for her?

"Miss Borg! It's me!" she said as she knocked. The

door opened under her hand. "Miss Borg! It's me, Dorothy!" No answer. Dorothy flicked on the light. The house was empty.

There was nothing left save the two beds, the chairs, and the dresser. Every book, every pot had been removed. "Miss Borg!" cried Dorothy, nearly weeping at the bare mattress and the empty hooks over the kitchen sink. She marched over to the dresser, looked at her reflection in the mirror, and stamped. Stuck in one side of the mirror was a long-dried palm frond. Palm Sunday. How long ago? Dorothy removed it. It crumbled into a hundred powdery pieces in her hand. She opened each drawer of the dresser. The smell of lavender was faintly evident. There was nothing in any of the drawers but a single straight pin.

In the wastebasket next to the bureau was a long-dried broken nail-polish bottle. Windsor.

Warily, she made her way back across the lawn toward the big house. I wonder what Mrs. Hoade would do? she asked herself, if she knew her husband's been cut off from his inheritance. At once Dorothy was glad for Mrs. Hoade. It seemed just punishment for Mr. Hoade's all-around awfulness. He'd paid Miss Borg well, of course. Now Dorothy realized that the ten thousand dollar cashier's check he'd given Miss Borg had been in case this will ever turned up. Miss Borg had Mr. Hoade over a barrel, if it did. On the other hand he had her over a barrel because he could easily prove prescribed medicine had not been given. He had the autopsy. Miss Borg must have been on the place taking care of Mrs. Coburg for years. Had she taken care of Jenny for a time too, before the Hoades had lived in South America? Jenny had recognized some German so perhaps she had.

Dorothy wondered if Mrs. Hoade would leave Mr. Hoade, knowing he was no longer rich, or would she go along with his plan, which would undoubtedly be to destroy the will? If I give the will to her, she'll at least have a choice. If she writes Miss Borg in Germany and lets her know, she'll be free of him. If I were Mrs. Hoade, Dorothy decided, I would want me to give her the chance. What a position I'm in! she thought. "Pride goeth before a fall," said someone in her mind.

The Hoades had come back. There was a single small light in the living room and one upstairs. The words *laute Anschreien* remained stubbornly in her mind. They had become loud-shrieking-at in a sort of English German. At any rate, they suited Mr. Hoade better than any English word she knew. So he had gone down there and tried to get the old lady to sign a new will, just in case the old one ever turned up. The unsigned new will was what had been thrown away the night she'd hidden in Jenny's cave. An unsigned space for a witness on an unsigned will. He'd pushed her over the line, kept her alive on drugs beyond her own will to live, and made her last days so miserable that Miss Borg had simply let her go in peace. Well, he was going to see! He was just going to see!

Dorothy's feet rushed noiselessly through the velvety grass; the fog had now risen to a height level with her knees. She felt as if she were walking straight through a cloud. She glanced into the living room ahead of her. The red student shade glowed on the whaler's lamp beside Mrs. Hoade's favorite reading chair. Everything looked peaceful. Upstairs the light was quite a bit brighter. Then she stopped dead in the fine cloud of mist that swept over the garden and up the trunks of the trees. The upstairs light was on in her room, and she knew she'd turned it off. Someone was in there. The envelope, saying WILL in that distinctive purple hand, was sitting right on her bureau.

She rubbed her hands on her dungarees exactly as she'd done before she touched the switch on her bedroom wall, as if, by this gesture, she could remember not doing it. She thought she saw a shadow move across the back of the room. Then she saw his profile, quite clearly, as he bent over and picked something off the floor. The fog, whirling around her now like a live creature, threatened to envelop the house, Dorothy, and the whole world around in its gentle, blinding embrace. Stuffing the will into her back pocket, she forced herself to move, to unroot her feet, to go into the house.

"Dorothy?" said Mrs. Hoade. She put down her drink and rubbed one eye. "We were wondering where you were. I was going to go get you. Jenny said you went to get your bathing cap?"

"Yes, Mrs. Hoade. I have something to show . . ."

"Dear, have you packed? It's time to go!"

"No, but . . ."

"Well, if you want to make your train you'll have to hurry. You have no time. Come now, run upstairs and get your things together. When you come down I'll give you *my* surprise! Hurry!"

"But Mrs. Hoade . . ."

"Hurry!"

I'll tell her in the car. I'll give it to her in the car, Dorothy thought. It'll be better anyway since he won't even be around. She made as much creaking noise as she could going up the stairs. If he was still in her bedroom he'd be able to slip out.

No one was there. Her things had been given a thorough going through, however. Dorothy threw her clothes into her suitcase in a jumbled mass. She had no time to change into her slacks or her traveling skirt and blouse. All the better for not being attacked in Grand Central, she told herself. Where was he? Was he waiting in the bedroom? She picked up the envelope gingerly from the dresser and then stuffed it into her suitcase with everything else. She checked her closet and drawers and the spine of *Ivanhoe*, where she'd hidden Miss Borg's paper just over a week before. For a moment she hesitated over her finished paperback mysteries. Because of the riding boots, the bulk was too much for the suitcase. The lid would not close. She scattered the books on her bed, closed the suitcase with one awkward knee on top, twisted the rope handle that Matthew had improvised for her, thanked God the hinges hadn't given, and made her way downstairs, her wet bare feet slipping in her loafers.

At the foot of the stairs, Mrs. Hoade held out the old tweed jacket Dinna had repaired as if it were a Paris original. "It's old, but it's still good," Mrs. Hoade said.

"I had Dinna mend the lining this evening. It's an old cut, but a real riding jacket all the same. The Harris tweed will never wear out."

"Oh, Mrs. Hoade," said Dorothy as she fingered the sleeve. The cloth was fuzzy and hard.

"And here's your check," said Mrs. Hoade, handing her an envelope and draping the jacket over Dorothy's shoulder. Dorothy slid the envelope into her pocket next to the will.

"Now rush out and get into the car," said Mrs. Hoade. "We haven't a minute to spare. The train only stops a second in Monastery."

Mr. Hoade's voice came from the darkness at the top of the stairway. "I'm taking her," he said, and appeared almost instantly in the living room.

"It's all right, John, I'll . . ."

"Give me the keys," he said firmly. "You're as drunk as a skunk."

"John! What a thing to say in front of Dorothy! I'm perfectly . . ."

"Give me the keys," he said more firmly, his voice rising. Then he turned and smiled in Dorothy's direction. "Dorothy knows all about us by this time, don't you, Dorothy?" he added.

Mrs. Hoade closed her eyes. He plucked the car keys from her outstretched hand as if they were a piece of fruit on a low branch. "Good-bye, Dorothy," said Mrs. Hoade. "I'll write to you, and I'll tell the girls good-bye for you. And thank you," she said, planting a shrunken kiss on Dorothy's cheek.

"Ready?" asked Mr. Hoade.

As he hoisted her suitcase into the trunk of the car, Dorothy made the sign of the cross in the air. This, then, is what it's for, she thought, but she wasn't sure it would work, any more than she'd been when Baldy had asked about it. The last glimpse she'd had of Miriam Coburg's portrait flashed into her mind as he started up the engine. She had been saying good-bye to Mrs. Hoade, but Mrs. Hoade's distracted, humiliated eyes had not focused on Dorothy. It seemed, instead, that the woman on the wall behind her was gazing at Dorothy with new vehemence. Was there some fragment, not of life but of will, left in that face? Mrs. Coburg stood guard over an empty safe, but her bureau drawers, her possessions, still retained the fragrance of her perfume, the living smell of a time before she was dead. The courage it must have taken to withstand Mr. Hoade's visits was evident in the doughty carriage of her body as the painter had seen it. Could a vestige of that strength live on like the perfume and reach out to touch Dorothy with more magic than the sign of the cross?

"Fog's coming up," said Mr. Hoade as he turned right onto Route 8.

"Yes," said Dorothy. He must have seen the envelope. He couldn't have missed it.

"Too bad you have to baby-sit on a holiday," he said.

"Oh, yes, well, I don't really mind. My sister hasn't had a day off all summer and—"

"Young baby?"

"Nine months. Ten," said Dorothy. A car whizzed by and swerved to avoid them.

"Drunken kids," he commented. "There oughta be a law against any kids driving. They cause all the accidents."

"Yes," said Dorothy unsteadily.

"Can happen to anyone," he muttered. "The most innocent people get killed in accidents."

Dorothy could not think well. The fog swirling around the outside of the car seemed to fill her head as well as the highway. She glanced sideways at Mr. Hoade's face. She could see no resemblance to Miriam Coburg's features. There was a more severe distance, however, between his manner and the manner that sprung from the old woman's being. The gentle hand on the dog's head, the imperious yet easy smile, had probably surfaced in some sloppy, twisted way in her grandson. Or had it been lost in the two generations that separated them? Dorothy pressed her arms close against herself, as she felt a single drop of water fall into the seam of her sleeve and creep frigidly down her side. She wondered how this Mr. Hoade had become a part of her life. He had come into it like one of fifty strangers emerging from a bus and then vanishing into a stream of other strangers. But he hadn't vanished. And he wouldn't if he'd seen the envelope. If there was just that chance, if he wasn't planning anything, if she got back to Newburgh, he and Mrs. Hoade would fade forever into the context of passengers in her life. In seventeen more minutes, when she was on the train and away, they would become members of the public at large. But there was no real possibility of his not having seen the envelope. Dorothy was tempted just to give over the will. What was he saying now? His words spun past her as rapidly as the white lines on the road. The hairs on the ugly maroon-and-green-plaid seat between them seemed to stand up in electric anticipation. "Accidents can happen to anyone," he observed, lighting a cigarette.

"I guess they can," said Dorothy.

"You never know when something's going to come at you out of the blue."

"No, you don't," Dorothy agreed. The lonely countryside around them showed itself in patches through the fog. No car had passed since the drunken teenagers. Shrouded fields, and black unmoving trees that had cheered her so often on her rides with Baldy, offered her nothing but their mute immortality.

"I hate dark roads like this," he said.

"I know what you mean," Dorothy answered.

"Not long ago," Mr. Hoade went on, "they found a kid near here. See that stone fence? He was around your age. Body all messed up and everything. Nobody ever found out who or why. Ever since then, you know what I carry?"

"What, Mr. Hoade?"

He leaned over and unlocked the glove compartment. Then he withdrew a small revolver and tossed it on the dashboard in front of him. "Your friend," he said with a smirk, "the fellow you thought was gonna be president of the United States? He always carries one. Never goes anywhere without one. Me too, now."

"Oh." This was a real gun, no doubt about it, smaller than her father's or Arthur's, but a real gun, nonetheless. Oh, why did I waste time over those silly paperbacks? she asked herself. If I'd come down a minute earlier, Mrs. Hoade would be taking me to the station. She'd read somewhere that fear had a smell to it. The back of her shirt was soaking wet. It prickled against the tweed jacket that she'd tossed on the top of the seat. Could he detect that? What was he waiting for? A turnoff? A thicker patch of fog? The purple thistle flowers gleamed in the headlights as they went by.

"The girls'll be going to camp next summer," he said. "Sorry you won't be around."

"Oh, that's all right, Mr. . . ."

"Hope you get a good job. Maybe something that pays a lot. You're Irish, aren't you?"

"Yes, I . . ."

"The world is full of Mick haters."

"Yes, my father says that . . ."

"Jew haters too. Everything haters."

"Better put that away," he added and he tossed the gun back into the glove compartment, locking it securely afterward. Then he slowed the car down and pulled over onto a patch of tire-worn earth.

"What are you doing, Mr. Hoade?" Dorothy asked, but he'd already gotten out of the car. Run, now! she told herself. She would run like a deer. She would fade into the pasture on her right like a ghost disappearing into a wall. She yanked the door handle, and then remembered it hadn't opened in months. She saw him pass the window on the driver's side. He'd taken something from the trunk, some metal object, long, like a wrench. He was shouting at her now. "What?" she asked desperately.

"I said turn the headlights to low beam!"

"What?"

"The button. The button to the left of the steering wheel. Push it halfway in."

Dorothy did as she was told.

"Thank you," he shouted. He got back in the car and threw the wrench up on the dashboard where the revolver had been. "Damn lights," he said. "They point downward. They're always slipping. I prop them up in their sockets, but the props always jiggle out."

The one light on the Monastery Station platform shone down on a single waiting bench. The station house was closed and dark. There were no other passengers waiting for this train. "I guess I'd better stay 'til the train comes," said Mr. Hoade. He dropped her suitcase at his feet. "Better get yourself some decent luggage," he added, laughing a little.

Dorothy didn't dare sit. She felt as if any noise or movement on her part might still alarm him into an unpredictable action. "Oh, by the way," he said, "you might have noticed your things were a little messed up, in your bedroom. Tonight, I mean."

"Uh, that's all right, I . . ."

"Lisa was in there."

A likely story, Dorothy thought. She could hear the whistle of the train beyond the near hills.

"She claimed," he went on, "she was only reading one of your books, but I guess she went through your . . . underwear for some reason. . . . I, uh—I, uh—Here's a five-dollar bill. I caught her with a . . . an undergarment and I guess it got ripped a little so this should cover it. There's your train."

Dorothy held the money against her stomach with both hands. The train wheezed and stuttered to a halt. Mr. Hoade had gone back to the car, a look of enormous relief to his turned back.

She tried to make herself comfortable in a single space beside a snoring man in overalls. She didn't dare try to get the suitcase into the overhead rack for fear of dropping it on his head, so she shoved it between her legs. The train was overcrowded. Children and mothers sprawled over the seats, disheveled, exhausted. Dorothy wondered how far they'd come and where they would get off. Who were these poor families? Members of the public at large.

I'll have to just send it to Mrs. Hoade, Dorothy thought. I'll put it in a mailbox in Grand Central Station. I need an envelope and a pen. Nothing will be open this late. Careful not to disturb the sleeping man at her side, she pulled a pen from her bag and Mrs. Hoade's envelope from her pocket. That was good. The envelope was blank. It did not have *Dorothy* written on it. She opened it and looked at the check. "Pay to the order of Dorothy Coughlin," it said. "Five hundred dollars." Dorothy smiled. Mrs. Hoade was truly generous. She slipped the check into her wallet. Well, now I'll do something for you, Mrs. Hoade, she said with satisfaction. Then she pulled out the check again. The name of the bank account was Maria Coburg Hoade.

It couldn't be, Dorothy told herself. She stared at the printing. If that was Mrs. Hoade's maiden name then Mrs. Coburg was . . . It couldn't be. Hadn't Mrs. Hoade told her in so many words that she'd come from a poor family? Could someone as sad and sloppy as Mrs. Hoade have been rich all her life? Didn't all rich people look like Vita, full of beauty parlors and suntans from the South of France, clothed in extravagant little thisses and thats from Paris? Yes, Mrs. Hoade had said she'd been poor. "She tells Daddy's Jewish friends she's Jewish and she's not"—Jenny's words came back to her. "She tells people things that will suit them, depending on who they are."

Mrs. Hoade's been cut off, Dorothy said slowly to herself. I can't send her this will. She'd destroy it. She'd lose all her money and Mr. Hoade too. Miss Borg would never know about it.

Dorothy looked at the check again. Maria Coburg Hoade. There it was. But hadn't Miss Borg said it was Mr. Hoade who'd come down and shouted? She slipped her hand into the suitcase. *Ivanhoe* was right at the top. She yanked it out and dug into the spine of the book where both Miss Borg's paper and her translation lay hidden.

At first, all the German words blurred in front of her. They might as well have been Chinese, despite the fact she'd looked up half of them. There at the beginning was the *Kreischen*, shouting, and the *Anschreien*—shrieking? she had written that night. Well, it didn't say one way or the other who had done the shouting. Dorothy began to hope a little. She stared at the part she'd so misunderstood: *überhaupt jemand in dieser Hütte gegen ihren Willen zu halten.* "Kept in hut against her will," she'd written above that part. At the time she'd thought it was a baby and the baby had been kept in the cottage against Mrs. Hoade's will. Now, of course, all this had changed. Mrs. Coburg had been made a prisoner on her own property. But by whom? Her eyes skipped down the page, through the *Autopsie* part, through the *Medikament* until they found that awful word *Anschreien*, angershrieking, once more. . . . *wenn sie abends herüber kam*, that followed the bit about no decent person could stand this screaming. *Sie*—the little word jumped out at her. *Sie*. She had written it down with its translation at the bottom of the page among other small words to look up. *Sie* meant she. When she used to come down here, something like that.

Dorothy crumpled Miss Borg's paper in her hand. Then she thought better of it. Naturally, it would have to be given, now, to the authorities, whoever they were. It can't be, she said again. It couldn't have been Mrs. Hoade. Mrs. Hoade's too nice. *Sie ist in ihrem Bad.*

Even Jenny's smattering of German had given her the meaning of that. She is in her bath. It came back now, as if to answer her last question.

Mrs. Hoade, who's done so much for me, and been so generous, Dorothy thought miserably. She jammed the paper with the nasty little *sie* and the will into the deepest compartment of her wallet. Mrs. Hoade, who got her best friend drunk and betrayed her, Dorothy also reminded herself.

A will was an important legal document. It was rather like having a fifty-thousand-dollar bill in her possession. She would bring it to the attention, naturally, of responsible adults. They would take steps. You couldn't take steps if you were not even fifteen. Nothing would happen to the Hoades, of course. It could never be proven that they'd kept Mrs. Coburg in the cottage against her will. "Miss Borg. Miss Borg?" Dorothy found herself saying, as if Miss Borg were on the train sitting right next to her. Miss Borg would be brought back from Germany. Mrs. Hoade had the autopsy. *Bewiesen.* That was a word that had caught her eye. Proof. Mrs. Hoade had the proof that Miss Borg had given none of the prescribed medicine that night. No matter how Miss Borg managed to explain this, it wouldn't look very proper in light of the fact that she stood to inherit. Miss Borg had not known about this will. She'd said she had no savings or inheritance. But who could prove she hadn't known? Miss Borg had let Mrs. Coburg die out of compassion, but it would be easy for the Hoades to say Mrs. Coburg was just about to sign a new will. Who could prove otherwise? At any rate, this was not for Dorothy to decide.

When she gave the will over to the authorities, through her father, through Sister Elizabeth or Reverend Mother, great excitement just might lie in store for her. THE GIRL WHO BRAVED ALL FOR JUSTICE! She might get her picture in the paper.

Dorothy began picturing herself at the lectern, after a glowing introduction from Reverend Mother. Bravery, courage! She could almost reach out and touch the eight hundred well-scrubbed faces that would be looking at her, envying her, waiting for her to describe her adventures, after they had finished singing the anthem that always opened the assemblies. "Holy God, we praise Thy name. . . ." The words of the old hymn sounded glorious when sung by hundreds of fervent young voices, when played with great gusto by little Sister Angelica Shipman on the huge organ at the back of the hall.

Dorothy felt her face breaking into a smile. A rush of tremendous pleasure filled her whole being until at last the young singers faded and became the weary travelers around her again. Reverend Mother's features slipped away and grew dim, until all that was left was Miss Borg's wistful, trusting little smile. *"Danke schön."* I won't bother you anymore, Miss Borg. *"Danke schön."*

What is lawful is what is right, Dorothy argued against that part of herself that said, Miss Borg will go to jail. She'll never inherit the money. You mustn't show this will to anyone, Dorothy. It will be easy for the

Hoades to prove—What would it be called? Criminal negligence? Manslaughter? If you bring it to light, Dorothy, the Hoades will have no choice. Dorothy's elbow found a minuscule armrest. She squeezed her eyes shut with her thumb and forefinger. If there was to be a GIRL WHO BRAVED ALL FOR JUSTICE! it would have to be followed by a NURSE GUILTY.

Just before she began to tear the will and Miss Borg's paper too, the one she was saving to show Sister Elizabeth, a voice screamed at her. "You can't do this, Dorothy!" It was Maureen's voice, a voice she'd thought so often was her better self. "You're breaking the law. You're taking the law into your own hands! Who do you think you are? God?"

She ripped both papers in half and then in half again, and then again until all that remained was a mound of white shreds in her lap. The window beside her was partially open. She let them fly, bit by bit, into the quiet fog outside.

She would never be able to tell anyone, of course. Not her mother or even her father. Certainly not Maureen or Reverend Mother. Sister Elizabeth? Sister's words came back to her: "God bless you, Dorothy, I think you'll find your way." Well, maybe someday when I'm old, twenty or thirty, Dorothy decided, I'll know what she meant by that.